# THE HELL-CAT AND THE KING

If Zenka's forthcoming marriage had promised love and not hatred, how could she have allowed a thief to kiss her—even to spite the king!

After the Golden Jubilee celebrations, Zenka is told by Queen Victoria, that she is to marry King Miklos of Karanya.

Furious at being forced to marry a man she did not know, Zenka determined to make his life a hell on earth.

But in the mountains of central Europe her feelings were to lead Zenka into unforeseen dangers before the King's insistent lips brought a happiness she thought she would never know.

# The Hell-Cat and the King

*by*
Barbara Cartland

**MAGNA PRINT BOOKS**
Long Preston, North Yorkshire,
England.

British Library Cataloguing in Publication Data.

Cartland, Barbara,  *1902—*
  The hell-cat and the king.
  I. Title
  823'.912(F)

  ISBN 1-85057-349-2
  ISBN 1-85057-350-6 Pbk

First Published in Great Britain by Pan Books Ltd. 1978.

Printed and bound in Great Britain by
Redwood Burn Limited, Trowbridge, Wiltshire.

# AUTHOR'S NOTE

The details of Queen Victoria's Golden Jubilee in 1887 are correct and part of history. She was in fact known as 'The Matchmaker of Europe' and nearly every reigning Monarch had an English bride.

In 1944 her known living descendants numbered 194.

The Crown Prince of Germany died in 1888 leaving the throne to his son, Wilhelm, who became the Kaiser.

He was a thorn in the flesh of Edward VII and because of his hatred and jealousy of Great Britain started the First World War in 1914.

# CHAPTER ONE
## 1887

'So many relations make me feel ill,' Princess Wilhelmina remarked.

Her cousin, Zenka, turned to look at her with a smile.

She knew that Wilhelmina always had something unpleasant to say whatever happened, but it would have been hard for anyone to find fault with the Queen's Golden Jubilee luncheon at which she had entertained over sixty of her relatives.

Zenka had in fact found it, after her quiet life in Scotland, very exciting.

The King of Denmark had sat on Queen Victoria's right, the King of Greece on her left and the King of Belgium opposite. The gold plate glittering in the centre of the table had given the whole assembly a golden aura.

'You would think,' Wilhelmina went on in her ugly, guttural voice, 'that amongst such hordes of celebrities there would have been some young men for us.'

Zenka looked amused.

It was well known that Wilhelmina of Prussenburg, who was nearly thirty, had for the last ten years been combing the Courts of Europe for a husband.

As she was fat, very plain and had an irritating, insidious manner, the Princes had a way of vanishing as soon as she appeared, while any overtures from her family on the subject of marriage came to an abrupt end as soon as Wilhelmina's name was mentioned.

Because she did not wish to be unpleasant Zenka seated herself on the sofa beside Wilhelmina and said:

'There are a few eligible bachelors in the party. What about Louis William of Baden?'

Wilhelmina looked at her scathingly.

'Louis William is engaged and is only waiting until after the Golden Jubilee to announce it.'

'I did not know that,' Zenka replied simply. 'Then it seems we are left with Prince Devanongse of Siam!'

'Really, Zenka, you are being ridiculous!' Wilhelmina said, 'I am sure he has a whole harem of wives already.'

'I should think that very likely is true,' Zenka agreed. 'At the same time I cannot believe a Golden Jubilee is a good place to look for a husband.'

'The Queen is known as the "Matchmaker of Europe",' Wilhelmina retorted. 'If I were brave, I would discuss my marriage with her.'

Zenka laughed.

'I am sure you are not brave enough to do that. None of us would be.'

She thought as she spoke that Queen Victoria was in fact very awe-inspiring and it was well-known that the Prince of Wales trembled when his mother sent for him.

She was a law unto herself and had even altered the rules appertaining to the Jubilee.

She had obstinately refused to wear the Crown and Robes of State for the Thanksgiving Service in Westminster Abbey which was to take place the following day.

The Prime Minister had argued with her and when finally in desperation the Princess of Wales was sent in by her other children to beg her to change her mind, she came out of the room precipitately.

'I have never been so snubbed!' she told those who were waiting for her verdict.

Nothing and nobody would persuade the Queen to alter her decision to wear a bonnet.

She was well aware that Lord Halifax had said the people wanted 'gilding for their money'. Mr Chamberlain had added that 'a Sovereign should be grand'. While Lord Roseberry, more scathing than the others, had averred categorically that the Empire should be 'ruled by a sceptre, not a bonnet'.

Whatever the arguments the Queen would not listen.

Next day she drove to the Abbey in her bonnet and gave printed instructions for her ladies to wear 'Bonnets with Long High Dresses without Mantle.'

Even so it had been impossible not to admire her dignity and her self-possession as slowly she proceeded up the Abbey to the strains of a Handel march.

Nothing, Zenka thought, could have been more magnificent than the escort which accompanied Her Majesty's open Landau.

First came the colourful Indian Cavalry, then the male members of her great family, three sons, five sons-in-law and nine grandsons.

The crowd were thrilled by the Crown Prince of Germany, golden bearded and clothed in white and silver. With a German eagle on his helmet, he looked like a mediaeval hero.

His relatives knew he was voiceless and whispered that he had cancer of the throat, and the Queen was deeply worried about the scandalous rumours being circulated by Bismarck and his spies about her beloved daughter Vicky.

The Service in the Abbey was long but very impressive, after which the Princesses kissed the Queen's hand looking, everyone thought, extremely beautiful as they did so.

Luncheon did not begin until four o'clock and was almost a replica of that which had taken place the day before.

Now at any moment, Zenka was told, there would be a march past of the Blue Jackets which the Queen was to watch from a balcony, after that there would be present-giving in the Ball-Room.

'Here comes Her Majesty!' someone exclaimed, and Zenka rose to her feet as the Queen came into the room, the silk of her black gown rustling as she passed through her relatives and guests to the window.

It was much later in the evening after a dinner at which the Queen had worn a sparkling Jubilee gown embroidered with silver roses, thistles and shamrocks, before Wilhelmina continued her conversation with her cousin.

The Indian Princes and the Corps Diplomatique were being presented and there were enough men, Zenka thought, in brilliant gold-embroidered uniforms or diamond-clasped turbans to please even Wilhelmina!

But when they walked side by side towards the Chinese Room to watch the fireworks she was still complaining.

'I hoped you were going to dance,' she whispered.

'Quite frankly my legs are aching from so much standing,' Zenka replied. 'Oh, look at those fireworks! They really are magnificent! What more can you want?'

'If you want to know the truth,' Wilhelmina answered, her tongue loosened by the wines at dinner, 'I want to marry a King!'

'A King?' Zenka repeated in amusement. 'Why should you want to do that?'

'I would make a very good Queen,' Wilhelmina replied, 'and when I look at the Princess of Wales's diamonds, I know how much they would become me.'

Zenka repressed a smile.

The Princess of Wales was wearing the most magnificent diamond tiara and her necklace seemed to flash like moonlight every time she moved, but she was also undoubtedly the most beautiful woman in the Royal Family.

Looking at her moving across the floor, Zenka thought she floated rather than walked, that there was something swanlike in her long neck, while her infectious smile made her different from everyone else.

Wilhelmina had as much chance of looking like the Princess of Wales as jumping over the moon, Zenka thought, but aloud she remarked:

'I think Cousin Alexandra has a lot to put up with.'

'You mean the Prince's love-affairs,' Wilhelmina said in a rather ugly tone. 'Everyone knows about them, but she has plenty of compensations.'

'I wonder...' Zenka remarked reflectively.

'I see nothing to wonder about,' Wilhelmina interrupted, 'and I tell you, Zenka,

16

I want to be a Queen! It is not fair that everyone else in Europe seems to have been married off except me.'

There was something so bitter in her tone that once again Zenka felt sorry for her.

'There must be lots of Kings and Crown Princes who are not here to-night,' she said. 'What about all those Principalities and Royal States near you at Prussenberg?'

'The Monarchs who rule them are all married,' Wilhelmina replied.

Zenka racked her brains to think of one who was not.

It was true that all the most important thrones in Europe were already occupied by one of Queen Victoria's daughters or grand-daughters.

She glanced round the Chinese Room, seeing Vicky, the Crown Princess of Germany; Alice, Grand Duchess of Hesse; Beatrice of Battenberg; Helen of Schleswig-Holstein; and a whole number of other royalties all of whom owed their position and the man who had been chosen for them as a husband,

17

to the Queen.

"There must be somebody," she thought to herself. Then aloud she gave an exclamation.

'I know, Wilhelmina...King Miklos of Karanya is not married!'

To her surprise Wilhelmina stiffened.

'I certainly have no wish to marry that man!' she said almost rudely.

'Why not? What has he done to annoy you?' Zenka asked.

Karanya was, she knew, a small country bordering on Hungary and Bosnia.

'He is a beast, rude, disagreeable and horrible to look at!' Wilhelmina replied almost spitting out the words. 'His face is deformed and he walks with a limp.'

'But what has he done to you?' Zenka enquired.

'He was here last year at the State Ball.'

'Oh, was he?' Zenka said. 'I do not remember him.'

This was not surprising since the previous year she was only seventeen and had been obliged to leave early.

'What happened?' she asked curiously.

'The King had to sit because of his bad leg,' Wilhelmina answered, 'and because I felt sorry for him I tried to talk to him, to make myself pleasant.'

She paused and Zenka could see the anger in her eyes before she said, almost as if the words burst from her lips:

'I turned away for a moment to speak to somebody else and I heard him say to a man standing near him:

' "For God's sake keep that fat little *Frau* away from me! She makes me feel worse than I feel already!" '

With difficulty Zenka repressed the laughter that rose in her throat.

'That was extremely unkind of him, Wilhelmina,' she said.

'He spoke in Karanyan,' Wilhelmina said, 'so I suppose he thought I did not understand—but I did, and I decided that I would never, never speak to him again.'

'I do not blame you,' Zenka said.

19

At the same time she thought she could hardly blame the King.

She knew how infuriating Wilhelmina could be and was quite sure the only reason for her wanting to talk to the King at all was that he was a Monarch and she was determined to marry one.

'I have learnt a great deal about King Miklos since then,' Wilhelmina said spitefully.

'What have you heard?'

'That he gives orgies—yes, orgies—at his Castle in Karanya!'

'What sort of orgies?' Zenka asked curiously.

'I don't know exactly,' Wilhelmina replied somewhat reluctantly, 'but Cousin Frederick was talking about them when he came to stay with us at Christmas.'

'I would not believe anything Cousin Frederick says,' Zenka remarked. 'You know he is a scandal-monger and gets most of his information from that horrible wife of his.'

'I am sure what he said about King Miklos was true.' Wilhelmina argued.

'The only thing I know about orgies is what I have read about the ones the Romans gave,' Zenka said. 'As far as I can make out, everybody got very drunk and tore their clothes off. If the King's Castle at Karanya is anything like our Castle in Scotland it would be much too cold to take one's clothes off, whatever else one did.'

She was aware as she spoke that Wilhelmina was not interested. She was still brooding over her hatred of the King.

'He has mistresses too-dozens of them.'

'That is not particularly surprising,' Zenka murmured, watching the Prince of Wales flirting with one of the more attractive of his cousins.

Even in Scotland they discussed his love-affairs, and since she had come to London for the Golden Jubilee Zenka had heard of little else.

Wilhelmina was still following her own train of thought.

'I heard Cousin Frederick and Prince Christian talking one day,' she related.

That meant, Zenka thought, that she was doubtless listening at the keyhole—which was something she knew of old Wilhelmina did at every possible opportunity.

'Cousin Frederick said: "I wonder what has happened to Nita Loplakovoff. I have not heard of her for nearly a year and she was one of the most seductive Russian dancers I have ever seen."

' "I believe she is having a wild affair with Miklos of Karanya,' Prince Christian replied.

' "He would pick all the ripest plums from the trees," Cousin Frederick remarked. 'I rather fancied her myself!" '

Wilhelmina paused for breath and Zenka remarked:

'I am quite certain that Nita Loplakovoff, whoever she may be, did not fancy Cousin Frederick.'

She decided she was bored with listening to Wilhelmina's complaints and instead spoke deliberately to the Duke of Edinburgh who was also standing and watching the fire-works.

'It has been a wonderful day, Cousin Alfred.'

'I am glad you have enjoyed it, Zenka,' he replied. 'I am afraid the Queen will be very tired, but she was pleased with the reception she had from the crowd.'

'That is true,' interposed Princess Victoria, who was standing near them. 'Mama kept saying to me how gratifying it all was and she was thrilled with her telegrams.'

Zenka saw that Wilhelmina was going to speak to her again and hastily she moved to another group.

She was related to almost everybody in the room. Her mother, Princess Pauline, had been English and her marriage to Prince Ladislas of Vajda had been a very happy one until they had both been killed by a bomb thrown at them by an anarchist.

It had happened six years ago and it was on occasions like this that Zenka missed her mother desperately.

She would have so much enjoyed seeing all her relatives, being part of the big family congregated at Buckingham Palace, even though she had adored every moment of her life in Hungary.

Zenka had loved it too, and at first she thought she would never get used to being away from the wild beautiful land to which she belonged and the horses which meant more to her than companions of her own age.

But her father's greatest friend, the Duke of Stirling, who was also her Godfather, had made her his Ward and taken her to live with him in Scotland.

There she had been happy, very happy, until two years ago when the Duchess had died and in under a year the Duke had married again.

As soon as Zenka saw the new Duchess she knew she had met an implacable enemy.

The Duchess Kathleen was only thirty-five, much younger than her husband. She was attractive and would have been thought extremely beautiful if there had not been the unfortunate rivalry of her husband's Ward.

It was impossible for people not to look astonished when they first saw Zenka and having looked at her once not to go on looking and find it difficult to realise there was any other woman in the room.

While she had her mother's small straight nose and fine bone structure, her red hair came from her father's Hungarian ancestry and her very dark green eyes were a heritage from the same source.

Her eyes seemed to fill her small face and combined with an exquisitely fashioned body her whole appearance was enough to make any woman grind her teeth with frustration and jealousy.

The Duchess Kathleen had hated Zenka on sight and it had certainly not endeared her husband's Ward to her when at the Golden Jubilee celebrations Zenka because of her Royal Blood took precedence over a mere Duke and Duchess.

Zenka had been asked to stay at Buckingham Palace while the Stirlings had been forced to open their rather dull house in Hanover Square.

The Duchess Kathleen found it impossible to forgive that in the Abbey Zenka sat amongst the Royal Princesses, and had been invited to be present at the family luncheons that were given both on the Saturday after the Queen had arrived from Windsor and on Sunday following the Thanksgiving Service in Westmister Abbey.

She and the Duke were present now to watch the fireworks, but she was well aware that it was only because of Zenka that they had been included in the few special invitations accorded to those who were not of the "Blood Royal".

As a number of the guests became somewhat tired with the fireworks, many of which were bursting out of sight, they came from the balconies into the Drawing-Room finding it more interesting to talk to each other.

The Duke of Stirling saw Zenka standing by herself and walked towards her.

He looked magnificent in his kilt, the huge

cairngorm on his shoulder glinting in the lights of the chandeliers.

'Are you tired, Zenka?' he asked.

He was very fond of his Ward and he thought, as did most other men in the party, that she was beyond argument a very beautiful girl.

'I am a little, Godfather,' Zenka answered. 'Are you leaving now?'

'Kathleen is tired,' the Duke admitted. 'It was so hot in the Abbey and we were rather closely packed in our seats.'

'The Queen must be exhausted,' Zenka said. 'She did not stay long for the fireworks.'

'No,' the Duke agreed, 'and she has another long day tomorrow. I suppose you will be accompanying her to Hyde Park?'

'I would hate to miss it,' Zenka answered. 'There are to be Military Bands, a treat for 30,000 school-children and a balloon.'

'Then you must certainly go,' the Duke laughed, 'but you will not be going to Windsor with the Queen?'

'No, of course not,' Zenka answered. 'As soon as Her Majesty leaves London I will come to you.'

'Yes, do that,' the Duke agreed.

As he spoke the Duchess came to his side.

She was wearing every jewel the Stirlings had ever possessed, but there was a discontented droop on her lips and her eyes when she looked at Zenka were hard.

'I presume,' she said acidly, 'that you do not intend to come home with us?'

'I am expected to stay until to-morrow,' Zenka answered.

'Which of course gives you a very inflated sense of importance,' the Duchess replied.

She turned away without waiting for Zenka's reply but the Duke put his hand on his Ward's shoulder.

'You look very attractive Zenka,' he said. 'The Prince of Wales congratulated me on having such a lovely Ward.'

'Thank you, Godfather,' Zenka smiled. 'I am lucky to have such a charming Guardian!'

The Duke smiled, then once again he patted her shoulder and hastily followed his wife.

It was early in the afternoon of the following day when Zenka arrived in one of the Royal carriages at Stirling House in Hanover Square.

She had enjoyed accompanying the Queen to Hyde Park and had been amused when as the huge balloon rose from the grass a child had called out: "Look, there's the Queen going up to Heaven!"

She had managed to avoid being paired with Wilhelmina either driving to Hyde Park or walking around there.

She knew it was unkind, but at the same time Wilhelmina, with her incessant whining and fault-finding was such a bore that Zenka decided she had had enough.

She remembered one agonising visit to Prussenberg when she had had to stay a month with Wilhelmina and her brothers and sisters and found them all equally unpleasant and tiresome.

She had never been asked again, mostly she thought, because Wilhelmina's elder brother had paid far too much attention to her and she was not included as an eligible *parti* on the Prussunberg list for their children.

Prince Ladislas may have transmitted to his daughter great beauty, but he had not been able to leave her a large fortune.

The European Royalties were very conscious where wives for their sons were concerned that money was more valuable than looks and a substantial dowry far more reliable than an ability to turn a man's head.

As soon as she had entered her Godfather's house Zenka sensed that something unusual was about to happen.

She did not know why, but she was curiously perceptive at times—almost clairvoyantly so—and although in Scotland they called her "fey" she seldom paid much attention to such feelings unless they specifically concerned herself.

Now in the dim, rather ugly Hall she was

suddenly aware of a feeling of unease that was almost one of fear.

Although it was a hot day she felt cold, and although she tried to laugh at herself it was as if, as her Nanny used to say, "a goose was walking over her grave".

She had for some unknown reason a wild desire to run away before she walked up the stairs to the large double Drawing-Room on the first floor.

'I must be overtired,' she thought.

She pulled off her small straw hat and pushed her red hair that had been flattened by it back into place.

Then in her pretty striped silk gown, which had aroused much admiration amongst the other Princesses, she walked into the Drawing-Room.

The Duchess Kathleen was sitting on a hard upright sofa by the fireplace embroidering in a round frame.

Her lips were pursed together in concentration as the needle went in and out of the canvas neatly and precisely.

31

The Duke was standing beside her with his back to the empty fireplace, and Zenka had the feeling that he would have liked to warm himself because like her he was feeling cold.

Then she forced herself to move forward smiling as she said:

'I am back, Godfather, and I am earlier than I thought I would be.'

'It is nice to see you, Zenka.'

He kissed her cheek and Zenka curtsied to the Duchess.

'I hope you enjoyed yourself with all your grand relations,' the Duchess Kathleen remarked, and it was quite obvious from her tone that she hoped nothing of the sort.

'It has been a great experience,' Zenka answered, 'and something I shall always remember. The Queen was really magnificent in Hyde Park. She must be feeling very tired after three days of celebrations.'

'She is made of iron,' the Duchess remarked and it was not a compliment.

As she spoke she glanced up at the Duke

as if to prompt him, and he cleared his throat before he said:

'Sit down, Zenka. I have something to say to you.' Zenka drew in her breath.

It was true then what she had felt. Something was wrong, but what it might be she could not imagine.

Again she felt that prickling of her flesh and her fingers were cold as she sat down on the sofa opposite to the one occupied by the Duchess and put her hat beside her.

'What is it, Godfather?' she asked.

'I had a short talk with the Queen on Saturday morning after she arrived from Windsor,' the Duke said.

Zenka's eyes were on his face, but he did not look at her and she had the feeling he was embarrassed by what he had to say.

'Her Majesty, as you can imagine, had little time to spare,' the Duke went on. 'She had flowers to inspect which had been left at Buckingham Palace—and very magnificent they were—and also she had to rest before the family luncheon.'

'To which we were not invited,' the Duchess interposed bitterly.

'We are not Royal, my dear,' the Duke answered.

'Of course not—not like Zenka!' the Duchess snapped.

'Why did the Queen wish to see you, Godfather?' Zenka asked.

She knew he disliked being side-tracked from what he was going to say and because he was not particularly quick-witted the Duchess always managed to confuse him.

'That is just what I was going to tell you, Zenka,' the Duke said gratefully. 'The Queen informed me that she has decided now you are eighteen to arrange a marriage for you!'

Whatever Zenka had expected to hear it was not this. Her eyes widened and for a moment she was very still before she asked:

'Why should the Queen arrange my marriage? There is certainly no need for her to do so.'

'You forget,' the Duke replied, 'that the

34

Queen was very fond of your dear mother. She spoke of her with deep affection and also of your father. It was a great shock to her, a shock she has never forgotten, when they were both killed.'

'It was a shock to me too,' Zenka said in a low voice, 'but I have no wish for the Queen to arrange a marriage for me, nor at the moment have I any wish to marry.'

'It is an honour, my dear, that Her Majesty should think of you.'

'I know that,' Zenka said quickly, 'but I want to choose my own husband. I will not be married off like all those other Princesses!'

She paused and as the Duke did not speak she said:

'I was thinking of them to-day, thinking that it must be rather frightening just to be told that you are to reign over some obscure country, perhaps one you have never been to, simply because the Queen considers it an advisable match to support what the Diplomats call "the balance of power".'

The Duke looked uncomfortable.

'Is that what the Queen said to you, God-father?' she asked perceptively.

'Something like that,' the Duke admitted.

'Then you can just tell the Queen from me,' Zenka said rising to her feet, 'that I have no intention of being just another spoke in the wheel of the British juggernaut.'

She walked across the room before she said:

'You know how we have always laughed at how the Queen manipulates everybody. You yourself have been amused at the way in which she has found husbands for her daughters and wives for her sons. Well, I am not going to play that game. I am not going to be manoeuvred in the same manner. You can make it clear once and for all to Her Majesty.'

'My dear child, it is not as easy as that,' the Duke expostulated.

'Why do you waste time arguing with her?' the Duchess asked sharply. 'You know as well as I do that she has to do as she is told. You are her Guardian. She is not yet of age and you had best tell her the truth right away and tell her you have accepted the King on her behalf.'

'Accepted? What King?' Zenka asked turning from the window.

The Duke did not reply and after a moment she said again:

'What King have you accepted on my behalf...I demand to know!'

'King Miklos of Karanya,' the Duchess said before the Duke could speak. 'You are an extremely lucky girl, so go down on your knees and thank God for giving you the opportunity of marrying a reigning Monarch.'

The jealousy was very evident in the Duchess's tone but Zenka stared at the Duke in dismay.

'It is not true! It cannot be true!' she said at last. 'Tell me, Godfather, it is not true that you have agreed that I should marry King Miklos.'

'It is what the Queen wishes, my dear.'

'And I know exactly why,' Zenka said.

'Karanya is, of course, important to the balance of power in Europe. England does not wish Austria and Hungary to extend their boundaries any further and Karanya is a buffer between that country and the Ottoman Empire.'

She paused before she said firmly, her voice ringing out:

'Well, I have no intention of being a buffer. I refuse...do you hear, Godfather?...I refuse absolutely and completely to marry King Miklos, or anyone else that the Queen chooses for me.'

She walked towards the door and only when she reached it did she look back.

'When I marry I shall marry for love, and no Queen or anybody else will persuade me to do otherwise.'

She went out of the room and with an effort refrained from slamming the door because she thought it would be undignified, and closed it quietly behind her.

She ran upstairs to her bed-room seething with anger.

How dare Queen Victoria think she could order her about as she ordered her wretched sons and daughters?

The Prince of Wales might shake in his shoes because he was so afraid of her and the rest might obey her without a single protest, but, Zenka told herself, she was different.

All the things that Wilhelmina had said about King Miklos came to her mind, and she told herself it was because the Queen could not think any other Princess would accept such a man that she had been delegated to him.

Well, as far as she was concerned, the Queen had a surprise coming. She had no intention of marrying King Miklos or for that matter anyone else.

As she had told her Godfather, she had long ago decided that when she married it would be because she was in love, and for no other reason.

She had seen and heard far too much unhappiness amongst her relations in the

Courts of Europe to have any illusions about so-called "love-matches" of Kings and Queens.

They had broken hearts and cried hopelessly into their pillows like everyone else.

It was only because they were brought up to put a good face on their unhappiness, to smile as if they had no secret cares and to perform their duty without complaint, that no-one realised how unhappy many of them were.

Once one of her cousins who had had her marriage arranged for her had broken down just before the wedding and told Zenka the truth.

'I hate Gustave!' she had cried passionately. 'I hate everything about him—his hot hands, his flabby lips, the way he drinks too much, his swimmy eyes when he looks at another woman, I am in love with Alexander, I always have been in love with him ever since I was a child.'

'Why can you not marry him?' Zenka had asked.

'Because he is a third son with no prospect of being anything else,' her cousin had answered despairingly. 'We were forbidden to see each other a year ago when they realised he was in love with me, but of course we have met in secret.'

'Could you not run away together?' Zenka asked.

Her cousin made a helpless gesture.

'Where to? What would we live on? We neither of us have any money.'

She had burst into a flood of sobbing before she went on:

'But I love him...I love him with all my heart! There will never be another man, and how can I endure the years ahead with Gustave when everything about him revolts me?'

There was no answer to this and Zenka had been a bridesmaid at the Royal Wedding with the crowds cheering, the guests saying how lovely the bride looked, and the newspapers acclaiming it as a "love-match".

Only Zenka had noticed the despair in her

cousin's eyes and the pain in Alexander's when they had said good-bye to each other before the bride and bridegroom set off on their honeymoon.

Just for a moment Zenka thought for both of them time stood still. Then Alexander had kissed the bride's hand and she had turned away with a hastily stifled sob.

'That shall never happen to me,' Zenka thought then. 'Never, never!'

It had somehow never crossed her mind that the Queen would be interested in her.

Now Zenka thought that when Her Majesty spent her time in the seclusion of Windsor she was like a huge spider spinning her web so that stupid little flies once caught in it had no chance of escape.

'I will not be caught!' Zenka said aloud. 'Before we go back to Scotland, Godfather must go to Windsor and tell the Queen she can find another bride for the horrible King Miklos who made himself so unpleasant to Wilhelmina.'

That of course, she thought was the solution. Why should Wilhelmina not marry him?

She had been trying hard enough to find a husband, and although she made a great fuss about disliking King Miklos the idea of being a Queen would doubtless silence her objections. She would accept him willingly if she could have a crown on her head.

'Godfather can suggest Wilhelmina as an alternative to me,' Zenka said aloud.

As she spoke the door opened and the Duchess Kathleen came in.

'I have come to talk to you, Zenka.'

'I have nothing to add to what I have already said,' Zenka replied.

'That remains to be seen,' the Duchess answered. 'You are well aware that your behaviour has upset your Guardian as it has upset me.'

Zenka thought it was unlikely the Duchess was in the least upset by anything she had said or done, but aloud she replied:

'I am sorry if Godfather feels uncomfortable because I have refused to comply with the Queen's wishes, but they should have consulted me in the first place. It was their idea to hand me like a package over the counter, doubtless wrapped in a Union Jack, but fortunately I have a mind of my own.'

The Duchess smiled unpleasantly and crossing the room sat down in an arm-chair by the fireplace.

'I suppose you have thought over this proposal before reaching this decision?'

'There is nothing to think about,' Zenka said. 'As I have already said, I have no intention of being married to anyone I do not love. You may not know it, but my father and mother did not have an arranged marriage.'

She looked at the Duchess as she spoke and realised this was in fact something of which she was not aware.

'My father saw my mother first when she was sixteen, at a Ball given for one of her cousins at which she was allowed to be present just for an hour. She was only a school-girl but he knew that he loved her and intended to marry her.'

Zenka's voice deepened as she went on:

'They had to wait for two years but neither of them ever looked at anyone else and finally when they were married they were blissfully happy.'

'That is an exceptional case, as you well know,' the Duchess said. 'Most girls have an arranged marriage in one way or another, and it is usually left to their mother or father to find an eligible suitor.'

'I am aware of that,' Zenka answered, 'but I think it is a horrible, barbaric custom. I intend to wait until I fall in love, as my father and mother did.'

'And supposing that never happens?'

'Then I shall just be an old maid.'

'Living with us in Scotland?' the Duchess asked.

'Are you really so anxious to get rid of me?'

'Extremely anxious!' the Duchess answered bluntly.

Her reply was a surprise and Zenka looked at her wide-eyed as she explained:

'Quite frankly I do not want another woman in my house, and as we are being honest with each other let me say that I do not like you—I do not like your character— and your appearance is disturbing, to say the least of it.'

'You are certainly very frank!'

'I see no reason for us to be anything else with each other,' the Duchess answered. 'You are not a relation of my husband's. He took you in out of pity.'

'He liked having me and so did...Duchess Anne until she died,' Zenka said in a low voice.

'That is as may be,' the Duchess Kathleen replied. 'But I have no reason to love you and you mean nothing in my life except an obstruction to my happiness.'

'I dare say I can find someone else who would have me.'

'The person who will have you is King Miklos!'

'I do not mean to get married.'

'That makes it very difficult,' the Duchess

said slowly.

'Why?' Zenka asked.

'Because your Godfather and Guardian has already accepted the Queen's proposal on your behalf.'

'Then he must say he has made a mistake.'

'Do you really imagine he could say that without making a fool of himself?' the Duchess asked angrily.

'He should have asked me first.'

'Do you suppose the Queen will expect a mere chit of eighteen to defy her wishes? This is a Royal Command, as you well know. It is not a question of whether you will or will not become the Queen of Karanya. You have been told that you will marry the King and that is the end of the matter!'

'Which I have no intention of doing,' Zenka cried. 'If I have to scream my refusal from here to Buckingham Palace, if I have to confront the Queen myself, I will do so rather than be forced into marrying a man I do not know and who is interested only in me because I am a representative of the

British Crown.'

'You ought to be proud to be of such importance,' the Duchess said sourly.

'Well, I am not, and that is all there is to it!' Zenka snapped. 'I am sorry if Godfather has got himself into an uncomfortable position, but it is his own doing.'

The Duchess sighed.

'Very well, Zenka, I had no wish to put an alternative before you, but that is what I have to do.'

'An alternative?' Zenka questioned.

'An alternative to becoming the Queen of Karanya which most girls would think a romantic position and certainly a very enviable one.'

'I think it is neither of those things. What is the alternative?'

The Duchess seemed to consider for a moment, then she said:

'As your Guardian obviously cannot go back to the Queen and say that you have defied him and that he has no effective authority over you, then your only excuse for refusing this offer can be that you wish to dedicate yourself to a life of service to others.'

Zenka looked at her suspiciously.

'What do you mean by that?'

'In mediaeval times,' the Duchess replied, 'a reprobate daughter, Ward or even a wife was always sent to a Convent. Your history books will tell you that.'

'Are you...suggesting...?' Zenka began in-redulously.

'I am telling you that that is your only alternative to becoming a Queen,' the Duch-ess said. 'I know of an excellent Convent in Scotland and there are doubtless many more in England. Some of them are enclosed so that the nuns lead a life of prayer; others work without recompense amongst the poor in Glasgow and other large towns. I am sure you will find it a very rewarding life.'

'Are you...suggesting that you will...put me in a ...Convent?'

'I am not only suggesting it,' the Duchess replied. 'I am telling you it is the only alternative to doing what the Queen and your Guardian wish you to do. The choice is yours. It is really of no interest to me which you decide will suit your peculiar temperament best.'

'I cannot...believe you are...serious.'

'I assure you I am very serious,' the Duchess answered. 'If you honestly think you can flaunt the Queen's wishes and disobey your Guardian without finding yourself quickly and speedily in the robes of a postulant, then I can assure you, you are very much mistaken!'

'You are...blackmailing me!' Zenka said between clenched teeth.

'For your own good—and mine,' the Duchess replied. 'I have made it quite clear, Zenka, that whatever your choice I shall get rid of you as I intend to do.'

'I cannot believe Godfather would allow you to...treat me like this.'

'Your Godfather thought he was doing what was best for you when he accepted the Queen's arrangements,' the Duchess said, 'and because he feels he cannot cope with your refusal to comply with this, he has asked me to do so.'

Zenka clenched her hands together.

'I hate you!' she said. 'I hate you because you have destroyed my happiness in the only home I have known since my parents died. You have made things miserable for me ever since you married Godfather, but I did not believe you would drive me, as you are driving me now, into an impossible position in which either way I move will be hell!'

'Hardly the way a prospective bride should speak,' the Duchess said scornfully.

'I could say a great deal more if I wished to,' Zenka retorted, 'and if you force me into this marriage, then I swear I will make the King's life a hell on earth! How dare he ask for a Royal Bride just because it suits his purpose and that of his country? How dare you make me accept such an outrageous and barbaric suggestion?'

The Duchess put back her head and laughed, and it was not a pleasant sound.

'You always were a little hell-cat, Zenka,' she said, 'and from all I hear of King Miklos he will just about meet his match in you. You should be two of a pair. I am only sorry I shall not be there to watch you tearing each other to pieces!'

'I have not yet agreed to marry the King,' Zenka said.

She was fighting, she felt, a hopeless battle in which she could not be the victor, but she wanted to go on fighting.

'Then do let me arrange for you to go into a Convent,' the Duchess scoffed. 'It will amuse me to think of you fasting, knowing that flaming theatrical hair of yours has been cut and hidden under a veil.'

She looked at Zenka and her eyes narrowed as she went on:

'Perhaps that would be the best solution. You will always be a trouble-maker wherever you go, unless you are shut away from the world, and especially from mine.'

The Duchess was taunting her and once again Zenka clenched her fists together until her nails hurt the palms of her hands.

'Leave me alone!' she said in a voice that seemed strangled in her throat.

'It will be a pleasure!' the Duchess answered. 'I will tell the Duke that I have persuaded you without much difficulty to agree to the admirable plans which he and the Queen have made on your behalf.'

She walked towards the door, her bustle rustling over the carpet before she turned to say:

'I shall so enjoy choosing your trousseau with you, dear Zenka.'

The door closed behind her and Zenka made a little sound in her throat that was almost like the snarl of an animal.

Then she walked deliberately round her bed-room smashing everything that she could move.

She swept the candle-sticks from the dressing-table and because they were made of china they smashed into small pieces as they hit the floor.

Then she knocked the clock off the mantelpiece, breaking the glass at the front of it and hearing the works make a sound like a groan as they came to a stop.

When she reached the bed she put up her hands to tear the curtains from the mahogany canopy, but they were tough and resisted her.

She pulled at them helplessly until suddenly something seemed to crack inside her and she flung herself down on the bed to beat her fists despairingly on her pillow.

# CHAPTER TWO

All night Zenka lay awake trying to think of how she could avoid the terrible fate which seemed to have descended on her from the sky without any warning.

'If only I was in love with someone, or someone was in love with me,' she thought, 'I would run away.'

Until the beginning of the year she had been kept in the School-Room, and it was only when they came to London that the Duchess made any attempt to entertain young people.

The result was that the men who had stayed at the Castle were mostly her God-father's friends and of his age.

The Duchess Kathleen was apparently quite content to be admired, complimented and flattered by older men; but as far as

Zenka was concerned they treated her as a child or else, because she was of Royal Blood, they were afraid to be too familiar.

'What can I do? What can I do?' she asked in the darkness and found no answer.

She thought that only the Duchess could have thought of anything so diabolical as having her incarcerated in a Convent.

But she knew she had in fact spoken the truth when she said it was both a refuge and a prison for those who disobeyed their relations or, like the lovely Duchess de Mazarin, offended their husbands.

Zenka was very well read and she could remember dozens of instances of ladies of noble or Royal birth who had been shut away for having offended their relatives.

She could imagine nothing more horrifying than being enclosed inside high walls, and it was her Hungarian blood which made her long to be free to ride wildly over the open Steppes with the wind blowing in her face.

'That was freedom,' she thought. 'I shall

never know it again!'

She was well aware that as a Queen she would be expected to behave with every possible circumstance, and tossing about on her pillow she told herself that the person who should suffer besides herself for this imposition would be the King.

If Wilhelmina had been right he was horrible, cruel and doubtless brutal, but he would soon realise he had made a mistake in wanting her as his wife.

It was hard to visualise what he was like except that Wilhelmina had said that his face was deformed and he was lame.

She imagined him to be something like the wicked King Richard II with a hump on his back, and she wondered whether if she really offended him, he would have her murdered.

Then she told herself she was merely being imaginative and such things did not happen in the nineteenth century.

At the same time something rebellious within her, something which sprang from her far-off Hungarian ancestors, made her swear vengeance and feel as if to achieve it she held a weapon in her hand.

'I will fight him!' she thought and because she could not sleep rose from her bed to walk to the window.

She looked out into the quiet darkness of Hanover Square and found it hard to visualise what Karanya would be like.

She had once had a Karanyan nurse called Sefronia, a sweet women whom she loved and who had only left her when she became old enough for a Governess.

Sefronia had talked about Karanya as if it was the most attractive place in the world.

But what the peasants enjoyed and what she would have to endure in the Palace were, Zenka thought, two very different things.

She suddenly felt cold at the thought of what lay before her. Then a fierce pride made her tell herself that whatever happened she would never be crushed or become subject to the man she was forced to call her husband.

'I hate him! I hate him!' she said aloud

and fell asleep saying the same words over and over again.

★ ★ ★ ★

The following day Zenka knew when she went downstairs that her Godfather looked at her apprehensively and the Duchess triumphantly.

During breakfast they spoke only commonplaces and when they had finished the Duke said:

'His Excellency the Ambassador of Karanya has asked if he may call on you this morning.'

'I am sure you have already accepted on my behalf,' Zenka replied.

'I could see no reason for refusing his request,' the Duke said with just a touch of rebuke in his voice.

Looking at his Ward he thought how lovely she looked despite the shadows under her eyes which had not been there the previous day.

He was sorry that he must make her suffer. At the same time he knew there was really no alternative.

In her position Zenka would have to marry sooner or later, and he was well aware of his wife's feelings on the matter.

Like Wilhelmina he knew there were no other Monarchs left in Europe who were not already provided with wives.

And he could not help thinking however much Zenka might resent the thought of marriage she was lucky to be offered the position of a reigning Queen, when she had nothing to recommend her except her looks and the fact that she was related to the Royal family of England.

The Duke had travelled a great deal when he was a young man and he had stayed every year with his friend Prince Ladislas in Vajda.

Hungary had always appealed to him. He liked the high-spirited, charming Hungarian aristocrats with their chivalry, their almost sacred ideals when it concerned the honour of their family, and their beautiful women.

He had known that they lived the type of life he would have enjoyed himself had he not inherited an ancient title and a great estate in Scotland.

When the Prince and the Princess had been killed it had seemed to him obvious that he should look after their child.

But he had never imagined the difficulties it might make in his own life until he married for the second time and realised how bitterly and resentfully jealous Kathleen was of Zenka.

The Duke was not a particularly perceptive man where other people's emotions were concerned, but he had begun to feel in these last few months that he was living on a volcano.

When the Queen had suggested that Zenka should marry King Miklos he had welcomed it as an ideal solution to his problems as well as to hers.

He had never imagined that she would react as she had and be so violently opposed to such a proposition.

Now he told himself, remembering how happy her father and mother had been, that he might have anticipated that she would demand love for herself also.

But where was there an eligible Prince whom she could meet and love in the same overwhelming, almost unrestrained way that Princess Pauline had loved Prince Ladislas?

'That sort of thing happens only once in a century,' the Duke told himself.

At the same time, looking at Zenka he felt guilty and that was an uncomfortable feeling which he did not often experience.

He took out his gold watch, looked at it and shut the case with a snap.

'His Excellency should be here within half-an-hour,' he said. 'We will receive him in the Drawing-Room.'

He looked at his wife as if for confirmation and the Duchess replied:

'I will tell the servants to show him up as soon as he arrives.'

'Thank you, my dear,' the Duke said and went from the room.

The Duchess waited until the door had closed behind him before saying to Zenka:

'I hope you are in a better mood this morning. You would do well to remember that anything you say to the Ambassador will be repeated word for word to the King, so I advise you to guard your tongue.'

'Do you think otherwise the King might refuse to marry me?' Zenka asked.

'I should not set your hopes on anything so unlikely,' the Duchess retorted. 'If he requires a British Princess as his wife, there are not many others available at the moment.'

That was undoubtedly true, Zenka knew, but she bit back the words that came to her lips thinking there was no point in starting the argument with the Duchess all over again, even though for the moment she hated her almost as violently as she hated King Miklos.

She finished her coffee and rose from the table.

'I shall expect you to be in the Drawing-

Room in a quarter-of-an-hour's time,' the Duchess said coldly. 'Try to behave with dignity. Remember the exalted position you are to occupy in the future.'

She was being deliberately provocative, Zenka knew that, and crowing over a fallen adversary in a manner that was almost intolerable.

Without a word Zenka went from the breakfast-room, picking up as she did so some of the newspapers which had been laid on a side-table in case the Duke should require them.

She opened them in the morning-room and found they were full of eulogies on the Queen's visit to Hyde Park the previous day, and how appreciative the 30,000 schoolchildren had been of the bun, milk and Jubilee mug with which they had been provided.

There were sketches of the balloon which had been named *Victoria* and of the Queen, accompanied by the Princesses, talking to some of the children.

'I suppose that is the sort of thing I shall be doing in the future,' Zenka thought to herself.

The newspaper also gave a list of some of the events that had been planned for the Queen during the Jubilee Year—a Review in Hyde Park with 28,000 volunteers, a foundation stone to be laid at the Imperial Institute, the presentation of prizes at the Albert Hall for the R.S.P.C.A., and the Battersea Dog's Home.

Zenka turned over the page and found the Queen was also to attend a monster Review to boost the Empire at Aldershot, a Garden Party at the Hertfordshire home of Lord Salisbury, and a Spithead Review of 26 armoured ships, 43 torpedo vessels, 38 gunboats and 12 troop-ships, with their crews totalling 20,000 men.

Zenka flung down the paper. It was too much—too impossible to contemplate—all that smiling, shaking of hands and listening to addresses.

It had been bad enough when she was only

a spectator, one of the Royal entourage, but to be the main figure concerned would be intolerable.

'I cannot do it—I cannot!' she cried.

Then she remembered that the Queen was compelled to attend many of the events because she had no husband, no King.

The Queen of a reigning Monarch would certainly not be expected to review soldiers or ships.

But there would be other things, an unending round of visits to hospitals, schools, concerts, exhibitions...

Zenka could see each engagement following the other in quick succession and herself moving through them like a puppet, saying the same things over and over again, smiling, nodding graciously, accepting addresses, listening to sermons.

'I shall run away,' she thought. 'I shall run away...but where and with...whom?'

There was no answer to this and slowly she walked up the stairs to the Drawing-Room to await the arrival of the Ambassador.

He was a good-looking man of about fifty with clear-cut features that made Zenka think that he had Hungarian blood in him.

She was well aware that at least half, if not three-quarters, of the Karanyans were of Hungarian descent, while the rest were Croats.

One blessing, if she could call it that, was that she would have no difficulty in speaking the language.

Since the majority of the words were of Hungarian origin she had had no trouble even as a child in understanding her nurse and she knew that once she was amongst the Karanyans again the language would come back to her.

The Ambassador however spoke very good English.

He kissed the Duchess's hand, then bowed to Zenka.

'May I assure Your Royal Highness that this is a very happy and auspicious day for me and my country,' he said. 'I am asked to convey to you the good wishes of my

Embassy and all Karanyans who are at this moment in London for the Jubilee.'

'There is one thing I wish to ask Your Excellancy,' the Duchess interposed, as if she could not bear Zenka to have all the attention. 'Why was your King not present at the Jubilee celebrations? He must have been invited.'

'He was indeed, Your Grace. His Majesty had a most cordial invitation from the Queen Empress, but unfortunately affairs in Karanya prevented him from accepting it.'

'A revolution, perhaps?' Zenka asked, a sudden glint in her eye.

The Ambassador looked shocked.

'No, of course not, Your Royal Highness. Nothing of the sort! Just some rather difficult domestic problems which His Majesty felt he must deal with himself.'

'You will appreciate that my Ward would wish to have met the King before anything so formal as their betrothal is announced,' the Duke said.

'I do appreciate that, Your Grace,' the

Ambassador replied, 'but unfortunately it is impossible.'

'Then I think it would be a good idea,' Zenka said, 'to delay the announcement until the King can come to England. He will surely be able to do so within a few months?'

She thought to play for time, but the Duchess was quick to scotch such an aspiration.

'A few months?' she exclaimed. 'But that would be impossible. I am sure Your Excellency will understand that if the marriage is to take place in Karanya, then the sooner we are on our way to your country the better.'

Both Zenka and the Duke looked at her in surprise and she went on:

'Presumably we shall travel by sea, and as I am a very bad sailor I could not contemplate embarking on such a voyage once the summer was over and the sea might be rough.'

'I can understand what you are feeling, my dear,' the Duke said, 'but there is Zenka's trousseau to be thought of and I cannot see that everything could be arranged in less than several months.'

'That would mean putting off the wedding until next summer,' the Duchess said, 'and I am sure the King would not wish that to happen.'

She was being very clever, Zenka thought, and she wondered wildly how she could insist on waiting another year.

That would surely give her time to escape, to think of some reason why she need not marry King Miklos.

'I am sure His Majesty would not wish to wait so...' the Ambassador began.

'Then my suggestion is that we leave for Karanya towards the middle of July,' the Duchess interrupted. 'It will be hot in the Mediterranean, but there will be the sea breezes and August is a charming month for a wedding.'

'It is far too soon,' said Zenka frantically.

'But why?' the Duchess enquired. 'It need not take us more than a month to get your trousseau ready and we could not possibly stay in London after that. The season will be over, the houses will be shut up, and everyone will have gone to the country.'

This was irrefutable, but in a final effort to save herself Zenka said:

'I am sure many of my gowns could be made in Edinburgh.'

The Duchess laughed.

'You must be thinking that Karanya is out of touch with the fashionable world. But from all I have heard, and I am sure His Excellency can tell you better than I, the ladies there wear the latest Paris fashions or order their gowns from Rome. Is that not so?'

She turned her blue eyes beguilingly on the Ambassador who was looking uncomfortable.

'It is indeed, Your Grace, and I will be frank and say that His Majesty asks that the marriage should take place as soon as possible.'

'You have been in touch with His Majesty?' the Duke asked.

'I sent him a telegram as soon as I learnt

from the Palace that Your Grace has acquiesced in Her Majesty's suggestion. His reply was very effusive, and he asked me, Your Royal Highness, to convey to you his deepest sentiments of respect and gratitude.'

Zenka's lips tightened.

She had no idea that anything could be done with such precipitate haste. She had been supposing that as Karanya was so far away all the negotiations would have to be carried backwards and forwards in a diplomatic bag by a Courier. She had forgotten that since she left her father's Kingdom all countries in Europe were now within close touch of each other by telegraph.

'If that is what His Majesty wants,' the Duchess said, 'then of course we must agree and we shall leave England in the second or third week of July. How do you intend we shall travel?'

Again the Ambassador looked uncomfortable.

'We were hoping, Your Grace, that perhaps Her Majesty would be gracious enough to offer the Princess accommodation in a war-ship. I am afraid our own Navy is very small and consists only of a few frigates.'

'I must make one thing very clear,' the Duchess said. 'I have no intention of travelling in a frigate! If it is to be a war-ship, it must be a comfortable one and as large as possible.'

She looked at the Duke as she spoke and after a moment he said:

'I had better have a word with the Foreign Secretary.'

'It would be extremely kind of Your Grace if you would do so,' the Ambassador said.

Zenka saw depairingly that everything was being decided over her head. She felt as if she was being swept off her feet by a tidal wave which was engulfing her and she was drowning in the dark green depths of it.

She wanted to scream out, to protest, but she knew there was actually nothing she could say, nothing she could object to.

Who would have imagined, who would have thought for one moment that her marriage would be hurried through in this manner, however intent the Duchess was on getting rid of her as speedily as possible.

The Duchess rose to her feet.

'Let me suggest, Your Excellency, that all these tiresome details may be left in my husband's hands. I am sure that after he has seen the Foreign Secretary he will have a solution to his problem, and all you and I need concern ourselves with is the wedding, and of course the bride and bridegroom.'

The Ambassador was obviously relieved and only too glad to accept the Duchess's suggestion.

Once again he made a fulsome speech on behalf of his King, reiterating how much pleasure his marriage would give to the people of Karanya.

Bowing, he would have left the room had not Zenka put out her hand to stop him.

'There is something I wish to ask you, Your Excellency,' she said, and for the first time she spoke in Karanyan.

The Ambassador, who was about to move

away, stopped and there was an expression of delight in his face.

'Your Royal Highness speaks our language very well!' he exclaimed.

'You forget I was brought up in the bordering country.'

'Of course, and may I say that I once had the pleasure of meeting your father and admired him enormously.'

'I thank Your Excellency,' Zenka said. 'What I want to ask you is, why does the King wish to marry me? Was it his suggestion in the first place or did such an idea come from Her Majesty the Queen?'

The Ambassador looked more uncomfortable than he had during the whole interview.

'You must forgive me, Your Royal Highness,' he replied, 'but I cannot reply to that question, because quite frankly I have no idea of the answer.'

'It is something I much wished to know,' Zenka said firmly.

'Then I will inform His Majesty of what

you have asked me.'

Zenka sighed.

'Do not bother!' she said.

She spoke in an exasperated tone and the Ambassador was about to leave when the Duchess said:

'May I say I consider it extremely rude, Zenka, for you to speak in a language I do not understand.'

'I must apologise, Your Grace,' the Ambassador said before Zenka could answer, 'but you will understand how gratified and delighted I am that Her Royal Highness should speak so fluently the language of her future subjects.'

The Duchess could only incline her head and once again the Ambassador made his farewells and left.

As the Duke escorted him downstairs the Duchess turned to Zenka.

'What were you saying?' she asked suspiciously. 'What were you asking him?'

'That is something I have no intention of telling you,' Zenka replied.

'Then you had better learn to have better manners,' the Duchess snapped, 'and we should start at once to purchase your trousseau, unless you want to go to your wedding looking like a beggar-maid.'

'Do not forget I can always wear the Union Jack!' Zenka answered.

She heard with satisfaction the Duchess stamp her foot as she left the Drawing-Room and went upstairs to her own bed-room.

★ ★ ★ ★

There was in fact very little time to get all the things that were required and which were considered necessary for an ordinary bride, let alone a Royal Princess.

Fortunately as it was nearly the end of the Season the shops in Bond Street were only too willing to concentrate every sewing-girl they had on providing a trousseau that would be written about and illustrated in the newspapers and magazines and would therefore undoubtedly bring them new customers.

Zenka told herself she was not in the least interested in the clothes that she was buying for the man she detested.

She had a sudden desire to go to Karanya wearing sackcloth and ashes, or such hideous garments that King Miklos would feel revulsion every time he looked at her.

But because she was a woman she could not help being entranced by the lovely gowns she was offered and the magnificent materials that were available in London because of the resources of a far-flung Empire.

British sailing ships all over the world brought in silks and embroideries, gauzes, muslins and cottons of a variety, quality and colour such as people had never imagined let alone seen in the past.

The Golden Jubilee had stimulated the imagination of the designers, and Zenka had found herself gasping at the beauty of some of the gowns which had been worn at Buckingham Palace and those which were now paraded for her in the shops.

It was not the difficulty of selecting a

trousseau which perplexed her, but of not buying enough to last her until her own Golden Jubilee.

Each gown she tried on seemed more becoming than the last, and although the Duchess, because she was jealous, disparaged everything, Zenka chose what she knew suited her and told herself that at least her clothes would give her confidence and foster her fighting spirit.

It would be difficult, she thought, to be brow-beaten if she was wearing an emerald gown with a bustle comprised of tulle and feathers which made her skin dazzlingly white and accentuated the green of her eyes.

There were white gowns and silver ones, gowns for the day in jonquil yellow, and adorable morning-dresses trimmed with broderie anglaise inserted with narrow velvet ribbons.

With the Queen's sparkling Jubilee gown in mind Zenka was persuaded into a wedding-gown glittering with diamanté which revealed her perfect figure and whose décolletage would, she thought be a perfect frame for the Karanyan Crown Jewels.

'What I really want,' she told herself as she looked at her reflection in the mirror, 'is a stiletto hidden in my breast and a dagger in my stocking!'

She laughed at her own fantasy, then it gave her an idea.

That evening when she was alone with the Duke after dinner she said to him:

'Godfather, you have let me shoot a shot-gun once or twice in Scotland, but I think it would be a wise precaution as I am going to Karanya to learn to fire a pistol.'

The Duke looked startled, but Zenka went on quickly:

'Papa always insisted on Mama carrying one when she went on expeditions, and as there are bandits and robbers in Hungary and Bosnia there are doubtless quite a number in Karanya as well.'

'I have never heard of any,' the Duke said, 'but I must confess I am rather ignorant about your future country.'

'I am sure you will think it a wise precaution that I should learn to shoot properly.'

'It is certainly an idea,' the Duke said, 'and I believe there is a shooting-school somewhere in London. I will find out about it from my gun-makers.'

'That would be kind of you, dear God-father,' Zenka said. 'I should feel safer and more secure when I am travelling about the country which I am sure I shall have to do.'

'The King will look after you.'

'Papa looked after Mama, but he still thought it a good idea for her to have a pistol of her own.'

'I see you are determined to have your own way,' the Duke said with a smile.

'It is a small request but to me an important one,' Zenka answered.

She changed the subject, but when she said good-night to the Duke she said as she kissed his cheek:

'Do not forget my pistol, Godfather.'

'No, no. Of course not,' he replied.

Two days later, despite the Duchess's protestations that there was not time, he took Zenka to a shooting-school.

She was delighted to find that she hit the target nine times out of ten and was congratulated by the instructor. Then to please her the Duke bought her a pistol small enough to be carried in a hand-bag.

'You must be very careful with it, Zenka,' he said. 'Remember, small though it is, you could kill someone with it.'

'I will only use it on bandits and robbers,' Zenka promised, 'or if I am threatened in any way.'

'I know I can trust you,' the Duke said.

He wondered why his Ward seemed more pleased with this present than any of those she had received so far.

As soon as the announcement of the engagement had been made in the Court Circular, presents had been pouring into the house in Hanover Square at almost every hour of the day.

They were mostly gifts from relations, although there were a few from the Duke's contemporaries.

As Zenka had never been to school and had lived in Scotland, she had few friends of her own age, and therefore the presents had little personal interest for her.

'More silver!' she groaned as another parcel was unpacked. 'I should imagine the Palace is well stocked with it anyway. Why do people waste their money?'

'You know the answer to that,' the Duchess said nastily. 'It is simply because you are going to be a Queen. If you were marrying a curate or some obscure, penniless soldier, they would not bother to send you so much as a post card.'

This remark, Zenka knew, was intended to deflate her sense of importance, but because she knew how spiteful the Duchess was it only made her laugh.

'I expect you thought the same when you married Godfather,' she said. 'After all, he was a Duke!'

The Duchess pressed her lips together and Zenka knew she had scored a point.

The Duchess Kathleen had been the daughter of an unimportant Scottish Laird with a crumbling Castle and a few unproductive acres. They, however, marched with the Stirling Estate and it had been easy for Kathleen to ingratiate herself gradually with its important and wealthy owner.

It was not surprising that, lonely and unhappy after his wife died, the Duke found it very flattering that this beautiful young woman was obviously enamoured of him.

In many ways, as Zenka knew, her Godfather was a very simple man and it was Kathleen who had done the running: so that he found himself, almost before he realised what was happening, married for the second time and actually very much in love with his new wife.

Kathleen was clever enough not to let him realise how much she disliked the idea of Zenka living in the Castle until she was installed as the Duchess.

Then everything that was spiteful, jealous and envious in her nature came to the surface and she found it impossible to hide her dislike of her husband's Ward.

Now because she was getting rid of Zenka and in fact enjoyed shopping, even if it was for someone else, she was almost human and at times quite pleasant.

'You might as well have a good trousseau while you have the chance,' she said when they were hesitating over an expensive evening wrap. 'All men, whether they are Kings, Dukes or commoners, hate spending money on clothes. Once you are married you will find these things have to last you a very long time.'

'But I can pay for them myself,' Zenka said in surprise.

The Duchess laughed and for once it was not a disagreeable sound.

'Can you imagine the number of calls you will have on your purse?' she asked. 'It is bad enough in my position. I have at least half a dozen charity appeals every day, so I suppose for a Queen you can multiply that by ten!'

She paused before she went on:

'I am sure the King will expect you to pay for your own lady's-maid and the presents you will have to give to your Ladies-in-waiting, your Equerries besides Station Masters and people like that.'

Zenka looked at her in consternation.

'But I have only a few hundreds a year of my own.'

'Then keep every penny of it for yourself,' the Duchess advised. 'There must be a Privy Purse into which you can dip your fingers, but you certainly will not be allowed to buy a new bonnet out of it.'

Zenka laughed, then she said in a low voice:

'I wish I could think of some really valid reason for not going through with this marriage.'

'There is not one so do not waste your time,' the Duchess said briskly.

'Suppose I ran away to America, and never came back?' Zenka suggested.

'You would not be able to afford to keep

yourself,' the Duchess replied. 'Of course you could be a shop-girl or perhaps get a part on the stage if you can act, which I doubt. Otherwise you would just have to marry an American. I cannot see that would be any better than marrying a King.'

'It is unfair that there are so few careers open for women.'

'You could be a nurse and have a woman like that old battle-axe Florence Nightingale bullying you,' the Duchess suggested. 'But it all comes back to the same thing. There is only one really reasonable and comfortable career for a woman, and that is being a wife.'

'Surely it depends who is her husband?' Zenka asked.

'All husbands become tiresome and very much alike after a while,' the Duchess remarked.

'That is not true,' Zenka protested, 'if one was in love...'

'Oh, good Heavens!' the Duchess interrupted. 'If one was in love! How long does love last in most marriages? Look around you! Look at the people you know or, if you prefer, the people you know about. How long has love lasted with them? A few months, two or three years, then they are stuck with the same boring face at breakfast, the same conversation at luncheon and dinner. It is bad enough in a Palace, but think what it would be like in a croft!'

'I think you are very cynical!' Zenka said accusingly.

'I am merely practical,' the Duchess answered. Some women have a fair choice of husbands. That is if they live in the right Society and in the right place such as London or Paris, and if their fathers are wealthy and noble. But for the rest there is perhaps only one chance of marriage.'

Zenka did not reply and after a moment the Duchess said:

'Because you are young and have a lot of silly romantic ideas in that red head of yours, you think I am being cruel and beastly. One day when you are old, even perhaps when you are the same as I am, you will be grateful to me.'

'Never! Never!' Zenka said but she did not speak as violently as she might have done.

'Wait and see,' the Duchess answered, 'and remember once you are married, once you have the ring on your finger, whatever the King is like personally you will still have a throne to sit on and the British Empire to support you.'

Zenka was trying to think of an answer to this when the Duchess went from the room.

She rose from the sofa to go to the window.

Could the Duchess be right? she asked herself, but she knew, if she was, it would destroy every ideal she had ever fostered in her heart, everything in which she had believed.

There was something mean and horrifying, she thought, in going through life grabbing with both hands only what was material.

She could understand what the Duchess had been saying. At the same time everything that was spiritual within herself repudiated it as wrong and degrading.

'Mama and Papa did not feel like that,' she told herself.

She knew that because they had loved her they would have wanted her to be happy as they had been.

She remembered seeing when her mother looked at her father a softness and tenderness in her eyes which had seemed to make her even more beautiful than she was already.

And no-one could mistake the look of adoration in her father's face when her mother ran to his arms as soon as he returned home.

'Have you missed me, my darling?' Zenka had heard him ask when he had been away overnight.

'Every moment, every second seemed like a century,' her mother had replied with a little sob in her voice.

'That is how I want to feel,' Zenka told herself.

Once again she wanted to scream, to cry

out because time was closing in on her and every hour was carrying her nearer to her wedding-day.

The Duchess had everything arranged exactly as she wished. The Duke had persuaded the Foreign Secretary together with the First Lord of the Admiralty that they needed a battle-ship to carry them to Trieste where they would disembark for Karanya.

They were to leave London on the 21st July, exactly a month after the Queen's Golden Jubilee.

The marriage was fixed for the day after they arrived in the Capital of Karanya.

This was not so much the Duchess's decision as the Duke's.

Grouse-shooting would be starting on the 12th August and Zenka knew it would be agony for him to be abroad when he might be in Scotland.

Because she wanted him so much to stay and could not bear to think of being alone with the King, she said to him tentatively:

'I am sure there is good shooting in

Karanya. You remember what magnificent partridge-shooting there was in Hungary.'

'There was indeed,' the Duke agreed, 'and your father was a first-class game-shot, but Scotland is the only place in the world where there are grouse.'

'I must find game for you to shoot in Karanya, then you will keep coming out to stay there,' Zenka said.

Her Godfather smiled at her affectionately, but she had the feeling that now he was older he found it a bore to travel abroad as he had done when he was young.

He was always busy on his own estate and with the many important official duties he performed in Scotland.

With an effort Zenka resisted an impulse to hold onto him and tell him she could not bear to be left alone in Karanya. Then she knew that even if he was willing to stay the Duchess would not let him.

They were disposing of her, getting rid of her as neatly as if she was an unwanted baby left on somebody's door-step.

She had a sudden feeling of loneliness and fear. Then she told herself that this was just the sort of emotion which would make her subservient to the King and make it easy for him to do what he liked with her.

'I will fight him,' she told herself again. 'I will fight him with every weapon in my power.'

It might not make her happy, but at least it would be some satisfaction if he was as unhappy as she was.

Wilhelmina had said there were compensations in being a Queen. She wondered what they were.

Somehow now she had finished buying her gowns they did not seem to give her the satisfaction she had thought they would.

At the back of her mind she could not help remembering that while she would be alone, a stranger in Karanya, Wilhelmina had said the King had many mistresses.

'I am beginning already to feel sorry for myself,' Zenka told her reflection in the mirror before she went to bed. 'That is an absurd thing to be! I have to feel strong... resolute. Fiery and revengeful!'

She gave a little sigh. She could not help feeling that all those things would be far easier if she was a man instead of a woman.

She could not imagine her mother being aggressive. She had been sweet, tender, gentle and very loving.

It was her father who told her tales of the great vendettas which the Hungarians had sometimes carried on for generation after generation.

He had also read her stories of the Hungarian heroes who fought valiantly against overwhelming odds and died with a cry of defiance still on their lips.

They had been brave and proud and would never accept defeat.

'Why was I not born a boy?' Zenka asked herself.

Then she realised if she had been, none of these problems would have arisen.

She looked at her reflection and it was hard to think of herself as a man. Her green eyes seemed to fill her whole face and her hair which she had loosened before going to bed was like tongues of fire in the light from the candles.

Her skin was very white and her lips were soft and curved.

She looked at herself for a long time. People had told her she was beautiful and she supposed it was true.

Then a thought came to her.

What would happen if the King found her beautiful? Supposing he came to love her? That could be her revenge!

It was a delightful thought to think of him at her feet telling her of his love while she was in a position to spurn him, to laugh at him.

He would learn then exactly what an arranged marriage meant and it would be a lesson he would never forget.

Then she told herself rather bitterly that even if the King did profess his love for her she would never believe him.

He had not wanted her as a woman. He

had wanted her only for what she represented. She was his safe-guard—his insurance against his country being overrun by invaders.

It was an insult that she could never forgive and never forget.

'A parcel tied up with the Union Jack,' she had called herself, and that was exactly what she was.

Not flesh and blood, not a living and breathing woman with lips to be kissed, with a body to be held close in a man's arms, but just a representative of the British Empire.

It would not matter what she was like—the King was prepared to marry her.

Zenka made an impatient gesture and her hair-brush knocked against one of the candle-sticks so that the reflection of herself seemed to tremble in the mirror and for a moment become obliterated.

She rose from the dressing-table and said aloud:

'He shall get exactly the sort of wife he deserves...a hell-cat!'

# CHAPTER THREE

Zenka from the deck of *H.M.S. Heroic* watched the ship nosing its way slowly into the Port of Trieste.

Standing on one side of her was the Karanyan Ambassador to Great Britain and on the other side their Secretary of State for Foreign Affairs.

A little behind her like two grey shadows were the Karanyan ladies who had travelled with her from London.

They were middle-aged, quiet, nervous and indecisive—in fact exactly like all the Ladies-in-waiting Zenka had ever seen in the Courts of Europe. They set out to please and they were far too afraid ever to voice an opinion of their own.

Looking at the port ahead of her and knowing that now she would say good-bye to the sparkling blue of the Mediterranean Zenka had an impulse to spring overboard and drown herself in the sea.

She had thought, because of the Duke's request to the Foreign Secretary that they should travel in one of the newest battle-ships, she would enjoy the voyage and have the opportunity to talk to the officers.

But she had in fact never had a chance to escape from the people who escorted her almost as if she was a prisoner to Karanya.

It was not only the Duke and Duchess who never seemed to let her out of their sight, but there were also the Ladies-in-waiting who appeared to take their duties far too seriously.

The ship, which was painted a rich combination of black and yellow, was a new territory to Zenka that she longed to explore.

She was fascinated by the huge yellow air-vents, the cat-walks at the stern, the canopy look-outs on spindly masts, the boats swung out on high davits.

She realised a ship was a world within itself

and she saw how the crew attempted to attain perfection with the decks scrubbed to the raw grain of wood, the brass-work polished thin, the wheel-house glass crystal as a diamond, and the sailors impeccably dressed.

The Duke had explained to Zenka that the efficiency of a Commander was judged by the appearance of his ship and its crew.

Swords were worn at sea and officers often spent their own money on extra paint or brass-work.

'H.M.S. *The Duke of Edinburgh,*' The Duke related 'has all the bolts on the aft-deck gilded and the magazine kegs are electro-plated.'

It was difficult not to feel proud of the huge white ensign fluttering in the breeze and Zenka longed to talk with the men who ruled the seas and were, she knew, the very heart and pride of the Empire.

But it was obviously considered quite improper for her to consort with anyone except her "jailors" which was how she thought of them, and now her journey by sea was at an end.

She would be allowed to thank the Captain and say goodbye to him but she had had no chance to talk with the smart young officers whom she had watched wistfully as they moved about the deck giving orders.

The Duke had once amused her and his wife by telling them stories of the different Naval Commanders he had met on his travels.

'There was Algernon Charles Fiesché Heneage,' he had said, 'who was known as "Pompo" to the Navy. He always carried a stock of twenty dozen piqué shirts with him in his ship and it was said that he broke two eggs every morning to dress his hair.

'It is rumoured,' the Duke continued, 'although I cannot be certain that it is true, that he takes off his uniform coat when he says his prayers because it would be unthinkable for a uniformed British officer to fall on his knees!'

The Duchess and Zenka had laughed and

the Duke had gone on:

'The most alarming Captain I ever met on my travels was Reginald Charles Protheroe who was known as "Protheroe the Bad". He had a black beard down to his waist and an enormous hooked nose, and a habit of addressing everyone as "boy", even his superiors in the Service.'

Zenka had clapped her hands with delight.

'Tell us more about sailors, Godfather,' she begged.

'There was Arthur Wilson,' the Duke said, 'who when he commanded the Channel Squadron used to ride out of Portsmouth Dock-yard on a rattling old bicycle. It is said that one week he entered in his diary: *"Docked ship. Received the V.C."!'*

These were the sort of sailors whom Zenka had hoped to meet on the *H.M.S. Heroic,* but instead she had been forced to hear the Secretary of State for Foreign Affairs from Karanya extolling the virtues of his country and the Ambassador speaking glowingly of his King.

Zenka had listened cynically, and only because the Duchess Kathleen was present had restrained herself from arguing or asking embarrassing questions.

What was the point of making herself unpleasant to these less important people? she thought. Her battle was with the King and she might as well reserve her ammunition until she met him.

From the sea Trieste looked impressive and she remembered that the port had been founded by Julius Caesar, although she was quite certain few people knew that today.

One of her Governesses had told her that it was a town of threes—three races: Italian, Austrian and Slav; three quarters: the old, the new and the port; three winds: the icy *bora*, the stifling *sirocco* and the *contraste* which combined the worst features of both.

It was the sort of information which because it was unusual had stored itself in Zenka's mind and it made her now look at Trieste with more interest than she would have felt otherwise.

The Secretary of State had warned her that there would be a deputation from Karanya waiting for her on the Quay, and sure enough as they sailed further into the harbour Zenka could see the bright red uniform and plumed hat of the General Commanding the Karanyan Army.

At his side she discerned a portly gentleman wearing a huge gold chain round his neck and she thought that this must be the Mayor. There were also a number of soldiers constituting a Guard of Honour and other dignitaries whom she could not indentify.

It would have been very exciting, she thought, had she not been growing more and more apprehensive about what was to happen when she reached her journey's end.

The mere thought of her marriage gave her a hollow feeling inside her, and at night she would lie tense in the darkness clenching her hands together and wondering frantically how she could escape even at the last moment.

It was a minor consolation to know as she

stepped into the launch that was to carry her to the Quay that she looked extremely attractive.

Her travelling gown was the blue of the sky, as were the small curled feathers that fluttered in her bonnet.

It was also amusing to know how much it irritated the Duchess that she should officially precede her and that she was the centre of attraction.

Zenka listened to an address from the Mayor in German, to one from the General in Karanyan and answered them both in their own languages.

Then they moved across the Quay to where the Royal Train was waiting which was to carry them to Karanya.

It was quite the prettiest train Zenka had ever seen. White with a red roof it had the Royal coat-of-arms, which was predominantly red, splashed on the sides of each coach.

When she entered the Drawing-Room which was to be hers she found it profusely decorated with white flowers, the fragrance of which was enchanting.

There were roses, lilies and lilac, and there was also champagne in which everybody drank her health and the health of the absent King.

The Mayor and the other dignitaries from Trieste did not stay long and soon the train was moving out of the town and into the stony wastes of Karso.

The mountains looked down on the feathery green setting of Trieste, but once they were among them the landscape was harsh and exotic.

Now as they climbed upwards from sea level there were small villages containing the first Mosques and Minarets of Eastern Europe and there were gorges and cultivated valleys, their fields filled with flowers which made Zenka think of Hungary.

Because she felt it was a reflection of the land of her birth which she loved so dearly, she ceased to listen to anything the people around her were saying and sat at the window staring out.

She saw flocks of sheep, the white oxen which pulled the peasants' carts, and occasionally there were bands of matted-haired Tziganes with their dancing bears lumbering after them.

For the first time Zenka felt a little excited as if she was coming home, then she swept the thought from her mind.

It was not her beloved father and mother who would be waiting for her when she reached Karanya, but King Miklos, the horrible, deformed man who was forcing her into a marriage she did not want.

As if they understood that she did not wish to chatter most of the party moved away into the other coaches and later the Ambassador came to her to say:

'We thought, as you would want a restful evening, Your Royal Highness, before you arrive in your new country to-morrow, that you would wish to dine alone with His Grace and the Duchess.'

'That is very considerate of you,' Zenka replied. 'At the same time, Your Excellency,

I think it would be very pleasant for all of us if you would make a fourth at dinner.'

The Ambassador was obviously very gratified and had no idea that Zenka was using him to protect herself from the sharp tongue and the jealousy of the Duchess Kathleen which was increasing every moment as they drew nearer to Karanya.

Zenka's coach was in the centre of the train and she was informed that the Duke and Duchess occupied the coach on one side of her, the General, the Ambassador and the Secretary of State for Foreign Affairs on the other.

Minor officials, aides-de-camp and equerries occupied a fourth coach, while servants, soldiers and several journalists representing the newspapers of Karanya brought up the rear of the train.

When dinner was finished and the Ambassador was withdrawing he said to Zenka:

'You will appreciate, Your Royal Highness, that this coach was designed by His Majesty the King for his own use. It consists, as you see, of only one bed-room and a Drawing-Room. If you feel nervous at being alone I will arrange for your lady's-maids or, if you prefer, a sentry to remain in the Drawing-Room after you have retired.'

'No, of course not!' Zenka said quickly. 'I would much rather be on my own.'

It would be a relief, she thought, from being surrounded by attendants every moment since she had left England.

The Ambassador bowed.

'If that is your wish, Your Royal Highness, it shall be obeyed. At the same time when the train stops just over the frontier so that you can have a quiet night's rest without movement, you will, I assure you, be well guarded!'

'If that means there are going to be sentries marching up and down all night,' the Duchess interposed, 'it will be quite impossible for any of us to sleep.'

'They shall not march up and down,' the Ambassador replied.

'They can guard us just as effectively at

a distance,' the Duchess insisted, 'and a soldier coughing, sneezing, or moving about will wake me immediately.'

'Then we must take care, Your Grace, that that does not happen,' the Ambassador said with a smile.

He said good-night, and Zenka kissed her Godfather.

'I was very proud of you to-day my dear,' he said. 'I thought your replies to the addresses which were made to you at Trieste were most admirable.'

'She ought to be grateful that you had her so well educated where languages were concerned,' the Duchess remarked.

'I certainly saw that Zenka had good tuition,' the Duke replied. 'At the same time she has a natural aptitude for languages.'

The Duchess found it hard to find anything disparaging to say about that and she moved towards the door of Zenka's coach only saying somewhat sharply to the Duke:

'Please help me, Arthur. I am always frightened in these connecting corridors in case they break away.'

The Duke smiled at Zenka and hurried to obey, while she went into her bed-room where her lady's-maid was waiting to undress her.

The Duchess had insisted on a Karanyan lady's-maid coming to England for the journey with the two Ladies-in-waiting.

Zenka had thought at the time it was cheese-paring on the part of the Duchess Kathleen, but when she saw the rosy-cheeked, smiling face of Fanni she had been delighted.

She reminded her of her Nanny, Sefronia, and she found she could chat to Fanni easily and frankly as she could not with the two Ladies-in-waiting.

As Fanni began to undo the gown she had been wearing at dinner, Zenka said:

'This is a very comfortable train, Fanni!'

'It is good that Your Royal Highness likes it. His Majesty designed it all himself—every little bit of it!'

Zenka was surprised that he had such

good taste, but the bed was very large and and she could not help wondering who had travelled with the King in the white and gold room with its rose-coloured curtains over the windows and a gold crown holding up the same coloured silk curtains over the bed.

The furniture was built into the walls, the carpet was thick and luxurious, and the King certainly seemed to have thought of every possible comfort that either a man or a woman could require when they travelled by train.

'The Palace also is beautiful,' Fanni was saying as she helped Zenka out of her gown, 'but at one time it was very ugly. My mother worked there when the old King was alive and told me how uncomfortable it was and how much the guests who stayed with His Majesty would grumble to the servants.'

'King Miklos has changed that?' Zenka asked.

'Your Royal Highness will find it magnificent!'

There was some consolation to know that

if nothing else she would be in luxury. Zenka thought perhaps the Duchess was right and it would be better to be miserable, bored or even angry, in a Palace than in a croft.

At least in the former one could get away from a husband one hated and be alone.

'That is what I want to be to-night,' Zenka told herself as finally she was ready for bed.

With her red hair falling over her shoulders she lay back against the lace trimmed pillows thinking that both they and the mattress were the softest she had ever known.

'Good-night, Your Royal Highness. May God bring you peace and good sleep,' Fanni said from the doorway.

It was a blessing that was almost identical with the one Zenka had known in her childhood and every time Fanni said good-night it made her feel homesick for the past.

She had a feeling that Karanya was going to be more like Vajda than she had expected and it would therefore bring back vividly the happiness she had known with her father and mother and the happiness which had been theirs together.

It would, she thought, make King Miklos seem even more intolerable than he did already.

All the way through the Mediterranean her hatred of him and perhaps, although she would not admit it, her fear had been growing until now it was like a great stone within her breast.

It was something hard, tight and heavy which never left her in her waking hours and which had become physical as well as mental.

Because she was in a bed the King had slept in, she felt as if his presence lingered there despite the fragrance of the flowers.

He was menacing her, encroaching upon her, telling her that she could not escape!

The train, Zenka realised, had come to a standstill and she knew that they had crossed the border of Karanya and now there was no going back.

To-morrow she would see the King and know exactly the type of man she was to marry.

She had asked the Ambassador when they were in London if she could see a portrait of the King, but he had replied that His Majesty refused to be photographed and any paintings that existed of him were out of date.

Zenka had been sure that this was because, as Wilhelmina had said, his face was deformed.

There had been a few sketches in the illustrated magazines linked with those of herself, but they were always taken sideways and she had the suspicion that they had merely been copies from a coin of the Realm.

They showed a man with strong features but they gave her little idea of what the King was really like, and she told herself that anyway they would flatter him as much as possible because Royalty was always idolised.

Zenka turned from one side to the other, patted her pillow beneath her cheek and told herself she must sleep.

To-morrow was going to be a long day.

She already knew that as soon as the train

114

started up after breakfast she would be expected to appear at the windows to wave to the people who would congregate along the line to welcome their new Queen.

Then when they arrived in Vitza, the capital of Karanya, the King would be waiting at the station to receive her.

'I will not think about him...' Zenka told herself turning over again.

But it was no use, quiet though it was outside and still because the train was not moving, she could not sleep.

The only light in her bed-room was a very small oil-lamp which was shaded so that it would not disturb her and was really no bigger than a night-light.

She had allowed Fanni to leave it for her because she thought it might be a nuisance if she wished to move about in the night and had to light one of the big oil-lamps.

There were two fixed at each side of the dressing-table, and one on the wall opposite the bed in which she was sleeping.

'I cannot lie awake all night thinking,' Zenka decided. 'I shall read.'

She looked around the bed-room and realised that she had left the book she had been reading on board ship in the chair she had occupied by the window as soon as the train had started off from Trieste.

It was an interesting book which told her about some of the legends and customs in the Balkan countries.

She had been reading about the Roumanians and felt sure that some of their superstitions would also be found in Karanya.

'I will get my book,' Zenka told herself. 'Then I will light the large oil-lamp so that I can see to read.'

She got out of bed, but because she thought it might be cold, she put on the satin robe that Fanni had left for her on a chair near the bed.

It was of white satin, appliquéd with heavy lace and with wide sleeves. It was very becoming, one of the many expensive pieces of lingerie that she and the Duchess Kathleen had bought in Bond Street.

As she finished tying the sash around her waist Zenka opened her bedroom door and saw that all the lights had been extinguished in her Drawing-Room.

There was an overwhelming fragrance from the flowers and she wondered if the King had actually chosen them himself, or merely given the order to one of his Equer-ries that the Royal Coach was to be decor-ated.

That seemed to her much more likely and she wondered who she should thank.

She thought of the flowers in Vajda where her mother's special roses and the great shrubberies of white lilac had been much admired features of the Royal Gardens and again felt homesick.

It was not difficult for Zenka to feel her way along the Drawing-Room to the far end of the coach.

The comfortable arm-chairs covered in velvet were all arranged beside the windows which were hung with thick curtains of the same material, blotting out any light there might be outside.

Feeling with her hand she found the chair in which she had been sitting and sure enough tucked away at one side of it was her book.

She picked it up, then on an impulse sat down and pulled aside one of the short curtains.

It was very dark and for the moment she could see nothing. Then looking up she realised the clouds which had covered the tops of the mountains were parting as if blown by a night breeze and she could just see a few stars glittering like jewels in the black velvet of the sky.

"We must be very high up," Zenka thought.

She imagined they had stopped just through one of the mountain passes which led into Karanya.

She looked out and listening she thought that even the Duchess would not be able to complain that the sentries had kept her awake.

She fancied it must be cold and the men would be muffled in their great-coats.

'To-morrow we shall be down in the warmth of the valley,' she told herself and again her thoughts shied away from the thought of what to-morrow would bring.

She was just about to close the curtains again and go back to her bed-room when suddenly she heard a slight sound.

She turned her head and realised that the door of her carriage was being stealthily opened.

Whoever it was he was being very quiet, and she wondered if perhaps it was her God-father who had come to see if she was all right.

But she told herself it would be very unlike him to concern himself with her at this hour of the night.

Then she drew in her breath as someone entered the carriage. A person was moving past her, walking silently down the centre of the car towards her bed-room.

Suddenly against the faint glimmer of light coming from her half-open door she could see a man.

He seemed large and ominous and Zenka was terrified.

She remembered how her father and mother had been killed and thought this must be an anarchist, a fanatic who hated the idea of Monarchy and would therefore either stab her to death as she lay in her bed or throw a bomb which would blow her to pieces.

Frantically she remembered her pistol, but it was in her dressing-case in the bed-room.

She could scream but by the time the Sentries heard her and came to her rescue she would be dead.

With a courage that was born of fear she realised that the man who by now had nearly reached her bed-room door would not be able to see her in the darkness and she said sharply:

'Stand still! If you move I will...kill you!'

She saw him stiffen, but he obeyed her and holding her hand as if she held a pistol because it gave her confidence she went on:

'Who are you and what do you want?'

She spoke in Karanyan but to her surprise a man's voice answered her in French:

'*Pardonez-moi Mademoiselle la Princesse,* but I was curious.'

'Curious? So you come into my sleeping-car?' Zenka asked.

Then as she thought she saw him move she added quickly:

'I have you covered and I am a good shot!'

'I am un-armed.'

'How can I be sure of...that? Are you an... anarchist?'

There was a quiver in her voice that she could not control.

'I swear to you, *Mademoiselle,* that I have not come here to hurt you.'

'If I scream the soldiers will come and arrest you.'

'And I shall doubtless be executed.'

'That was a risk you must have known you

were running before you came here.'

There was silence. Then Zenka said:

'I want to know the truth...why did you come?'

'May I suggest something?' the Frenchman asked.

'What is it?' Zenka enquired.

'If you wish me to answer your questions, *Mademoiselle*—and I am quite prepared to do so—it is a mistake for me to be so far away from you. Someone outside may hear us talking and wonder who is with you.'

Zenka saw the reasoning in this and after thinking about it she said:

'Turn round slowly...very slowly. Remember I have you covered.'

As she spoke she pulled the curtains she had drawn back again and prayed that he might not realise even though there was no light from the window that she had nothing in her hand.

She could still just see his silhouette.

'Come two steps forward!' she ordered.

He complied and she said:

'One more. Now sit down in the chair that is nearest to you.'

He obeyed her.

He was only a little distance away and if they spoke softly their voices would not be heard outside.

'I am very grateful, *Mademoiselle*, that you are trusting me,' the Frenchman said.

'I do not trust you in the least!' Zenka contradicted. 'I just do not wish to be responsible for your death unless there is good reason for it.'

'Let me say again I am not an anarchist. I have no wish to hurt in any way the bride of the King. I just wished to look at her.'

'I have never heard anything so impertinent!' Zenka exclaimed. 'Besides, why the hurry? You will see me to-morrow.'

'I found it difficult to wait for to-morrow.'

'You can hardly expect me to believe that!'

Then she gave an exclamation.

'I know...you are a thief!'

There was silence.

Because he did not answer she asked:

'Is that true? You are a thief?'

'Perhaps.'

'So that is why you came here...to steal my jewels. I expect there have been descriptions of them in the newspapers.'

'That is certainly true—the descriptions, I mean.'

'Well, as far as I am concerned,' Zenka said without thinking, 'you can have them!'

Only after she had spoken did she realise that it was something she should not have said.

It was indiscreet to say the very least of it. Then she told herself it was of no consequence; for if he repeated her words no-one would believe that she had sat alone talking with a man who was a thief.

'Why do you say that?' the Frenchman enquired.

'It is something I should not have said,' Zenka replied.

'But we are being truthful with each other. Perhaps that is why...'

'I am asking the questions,' Zenka interposed. 'I asked why you were a thief.'

She felt, although she could not see him, that he smiled.

'Because it is exciting, adventurous and of course dangerous.'

Zenka gave a little sigh.

'I can understand that, but one day you will be caught.'

'That is a risk I must take. It is a waste of one's life to be bored and I find it can be very monotonous if I take no risks.'

'That is where men are so lucky,' Zenka said almost as if she was speaking to herself.

'Because they can take risks?'

'Because so many careers, even that of being a thief, are open to them.'

'Women are very successful thieves.'

'They are? I have never heard of one.'

'They steal hearts!'

Zenka laughed.

'You say that because you are a Frenchman.'

'And Frenchmen, of course, are always pre-occupied with love.'

There was almost a sarcastic note in his voice.

Zenka laughed again.

'But, of course, that is traditional.'

'I can assure you, *Mademoiselle,* that men of other nationalities feel the same.'

Zenka suddenly thought this was a very unusual and indeed reprehensible conversation to be having with a man who had come into her carriage to steal her possessions.

'We were talking about you,' she said. 'Surely you can find something better to do than steal what belongs to other people?'

'I much prefer to talk about you, *Mademoiselle,*' the Frenchman replied. 'Is your heart beating more quickly because to-morrow you are to meet the man you are to marry?'

'That is not the sort of question you should ask me, nor one I have any intention of answering,' Zenka replied sharply. 'As I have already said I think you are very impertinent and perhaps I should be wise to call the sentries and have you put into custody.'

He did not answer and after a moment she said:

'I dare say I have enough authority to prevent you from being shot, although you will undoubtedly get a long term of imprisonment.'

'It would please you to think of me languishing in a cell?'

'It should be a matter of complete...indifference to me.'

'But instead,' the Frenchman said quietly, 'it would worry and perhaps distress you. After all, I have done you no harm.'

'That is only because I stopped you from doing whatever it was you intended to do.'

'I promise you that what I intended doing would not have hurt you in any way.'

'How can I be sure of that?'

'Because I give you my word.'

'The word of a thief?'

'As you say—the word of a thief, but even thieves have a code of honour.'

'Do they?' Zenka asked interestedly. 'Yes, I suppose criminals are loyal to one another.

They never give one another away to the Police, for one thing.'

'That is a popular fallacy which is not based on fact,' the Frenchman said.

'Then you are claiming that you are more honourable than your colleagues?'

'I have none—I work alone.'

'What do you do with the things you steal?' Zenka enquired.

'It depends what they are. I suppose you would really like me to tell you that I am a French Robin Hood taking from the rich to give to the poor. It would make this whole episode seem much more romantic.'

'There is nothing romantic about it!' Zenka snapped.

'On the contary,' the Frenchman said, 'I think it is undoubtedly the most romantic thing that has ever happened to me.'

He paused before he continued:

'Just think of it, *Mademoiselle*, here I am a thief, who is clever enough to climb into your carriage without being seen, sitting in the darkness talking to a very beautiful

Princess, the place scented with the fragrance of flowers, and though we cannot see each other I feel we have a great deal in common.'

'Why should you think that?' Zenka asked.

'Because there is something in your voice and in the aura that comes with you that unites with something in me and makes me feel that we have met before, perhaps in some previous existence.'

'Do you really believe that?'

'I swear to you on a thief's honour that I believe it, as I believe in God!'

There was something solemn in the way he spoke which made Zenka feel that perhaps he was right, and in the darkness something magnetic passed between them which she could not explain. Then she said hastily:

'I will forgive you for coming here, but now I think you ought to go.'

'The night is still young,' the Frenchman answered. 'We may never get a chance of speaking to each other like this again, but

I shall always remember how beautiful you are.'

'You cannot see me,' Zenka protested.

'I can see you with my soul and I know you are beautiful. I know too, that like me you are a rebel. You are fighting a lone battle. I only wish I could fight it with you.'

'How do you know I am...fighting?' Zenka asked.

She felt almost as if the Frenchman was hypnotising her, and although she knew it was wrong and utterly indefensible for her to continue to talk to him she could not force herself to send him away.

'I can tell by the note in your voice that you are on the defensive,' the Frenchman said. 'You are perturbed, perhaps angry, and also resentful.'

'How can you know these things?'

'It is easier to sense what somebody is thinking and feeling, and indeed what they are, when one is in the dark. Then like a blind man you use your extra senses—those which are forgotten in the day-time when we use our eyes instead of our instinct.'

His voice deepened as he said slowly:

'The eyes can see what is on the surface, but they seldom look deeper than the outer veneer under which people try to hide their real feelings.'

Zenka drew in her breath before she said:

'Because I am half-Hungarian I know that what you are saying is true, but the English part of me tells me that I should not listen to you and should declare that you are talking complete and utter nonsense!'

'Not being particularly interested in the English,' the Frenchman replied, 'I am talking, Princess, to your Hungarian heart, which knows that what I am saying is the truth.'

'You...frighten me.'

'I do not believe that. You are very brave. All Hungarians are.'

'That is what I tell myself I must be...but it is not...easy.'

'Nothing is really easy in life,' the Frenchman said, 'and you know as well as I do that real bravery lies in facing what has to be faced when one is most afraid.'

Zenka clasped her hands together in her lap.

'I am...afraid,' she said in a very small voice, 'but I would not...confess it to anybody else except...you.'

'You can say that because I am anonymous —a voice which, like your conscience, you listen to in the dark and forget when it is light again.'

'No, I shall not forget,' Zenka said. 'I think, because I have talked to you, I am not as afraid as I was a little while ago. That was why I could not sleep...because I was... afraid.'

'If I tell you that things are never as bad as we anticipate, especially in the darkness of the night, you will not believe me,' the Frenchman said, 'but it happens to be true.'

'You have found that?'

'Yes, indeed, and I have often found that things turn out for the best in life when one does not expect it at the time.'

'What I must…do could…not be the best for…me.' Zenka murmured.

'How can you be sure of that? If you could look into a crystal ball and see yourself in five—ten—fifteen years time, you would find that what has seemed now to be an insurmountable obstacle has actually been a stepping-stone to something better and far more pleasant than you ever imagined.'

'Those are exactly the sort of platitudes that other people utter,' Zenka said crossly.

'They are not platitudes,' the Frenchman protested. 'I am speaking of what I have experienced myself in my own life.'

'A life of adventure, a life of choice. You have done what you wanted to do. Do you suppose that sort of opportunity is open to me? Of course not, because I am a… woman!'

'Would you like to have been a man?'

'Of course I would! Why can I not be like you instead of which I have…'

She stopped because she knew she was going to be indiscreet.

133

'I should not be talking to you like this,' she added.

'Why not?' the Frenchman enquired. 'When things are bottled up inside us it is always better to talk about them and see them in their proper perspective.'

'Another platitude!'

'You are determined to wallow in your misery.'

Zenka felt herself stung as if he had suddenly struck her.

'That is not true!' she said angrily. 'You have made me say things I did not wish to say, I am not wallowing...I am fighting. If I sink, drown or disappear...I will do it defiantly...and I will fight and go on fighting until I cannot think or feel any more!'

'Bravo!'

There was a sudden warmth in his voice as he went on:

'That is how I would like to think of you! That is how you should be; proud, brave, and of course, very beautiful!'

Zenka gave a little laugh.

'I believe you deliberately provoked me into that outburst!'

'That is intelligent of you.'

'I *am* intelligent!'

'I am well aware of that, and now, because I think you should go to sleep, I must leave you, *Mademoiselle la Princesse.*'

Zenka was still for a moment, then she said:

'Do you wish to take my jewels with you?'

'Would you give them to me?'

'I cannot prevent you taking them.'

Then she realised she had given herself away.

'I was not really frightened of that imaginary weapon,' he said.

'You knew I was not pointing a pistol at you? But how?'

'Because ladies do not usually walk about in their nightgowns with a pistol in their hands.'

In the darkness Zenka blushed.

It was inconceivable that she had sat there for so long with so little on, talking to a stranger who was also a thief.

As if he knew she was embarrassed the Frenchman said:

'No, I do not want your jewellery. I have had so much more than I came for or imagined I would find when I entered your carriage.'

'That is a flattering thing to say.'

'It is the truth.'

Zenka thought for a moment, then she said:

'All the same I would like to give you something.'

'I am only too willing to accept anything you care to *give* me.'

He accentuated the verb.

'Then will you wait here for a moment and not move until I return?' Zenka asked.

'Of course!'

She rose to her feet and keeping her eyes on the faint light coming through the open door of her bed-room walked without stumbling down the centre of the car into the room which it seemed to her she had left a long time ago.

She picked up her jewel-case which was lying at the side of the dressing-table and put it on the bed.

She opened it and she could see the sparkle of diamonds and the gleam of sapphires, all of which had been wedding presents given to her by her relatives.

There was a diamond brooch set like a spray of flowers from the Queen, a necklace of sapphires from the Duke, and innumerable brooches, rings and bracelets sent to her from her cousins in almost every country in Europe.

She had hated each one as she had unpacked it.

As the Duchess said, she had felt they were given to her only because she was marrying a King and she would certainly not have received anything a tenth as valuable had her bridegroom held any other rank.

It would be amusing, she thought, if the thief took them away and she arrived empty-handed at Vitza.

Then in a tray beneath, which contained the brooches, she found what she sought.

It was a small leather case and it held the present that the Duchess had insisted she should buy for the King.

She had not wished to give him anything—in fact she was determined not to do so—but the Duchess had been clever enough to take the Ambassador with them to a Jeweller in Bond Street where she had forced Zenka into choosing a pair of cuff-links for her future husband.

The Duchess had let her imagination run riot and had insisted on one link of each pair bearing a "Z" in diamonds and the other an "M" surmounted by a crown.

It had been a very expensive present and Zenka had begrudged every penny she had had to pay for it.

Now as she took the box out of her jewel-case she thought with a little smile that the King would lose his present, but the thief, because she had enjoyed being with him, would benefit.

Leaving her jewel-case on the bed she walked back into the carriage.

It was more difficult to find her way with the light behind her. Then she bumped into him and found he was waiting where she had left him, but now he was standing.

She put out her free hand to steady herself and touched his chest. He covered it with his own hand.

'I am...sorry,' Zenka said hastily, 'I could not...see you.'

He took his hand from hers and now she held out towards him the leather case which contained the cuff-links.

'Why do you wish to give me a present?' he asked.

'It is something you cannot sell: it might be dangerous for you to do so. But I would like you to keep it and sometimes think of our conversation to-night.'

'It would be impossible for me to forget it even if I wished to do so.'

He took the case from her and put it in his pocket.

139

'You know what I want to wish you, Princess,' he said quietly, 'happiness in the future-great happiness!'

'That will be impossible! Just wish that I may be brave and have courage.'

'I wish you to have everything that you wish for yourself,' the Frenchman said. 'And now may I ask for another present—something far more important that what you have already given me?'

'Another present? What...can that...be?' Zenka questioned and it seemed to her that her voice sounded strange.

Because she was so close to him she thought she could almost feel the warmth of him.

'I have a feeling, although I may be wrong, that you have never been kissed,' the Frenchman said. 'I want more than I have ever wanted anything in my life to be the first man to touch your lips.'

Zenka was very still, then she thought of the King and her feelings of rebellion joined with something else she did not understand within herself.

This would be part of her revenge against her future husband she thought. At the same time the darkness and the close proximity of the Frenchman swept away all reason and caution.

She was not certain whether she moved first or he did. She only knew that suddenly his arms were round her.

For a moment she felt afraid, then his lips came down on hers and she felt him draw her closer and still closer against him and his mouth was possessive, insistent, and in a way demanding.

She felt suddenly very weak, soft and yielding.

She had no idea that a man's lips could hold a woman's captive so that it was impossible to move and almost impossible to breathe.

Then the sensation such as she had never known seemed to rise up inside her, to sweep away the hard stone within her breast, moving upwards into her throat until it reached her lips.

It was so beautiful, so ecstatic, so perfect, that it was hard to know what she felt, and yet she knew that it was different from anything she had imagined a kiss could be like.

It was altogether wonderful, and without really meaning to do so she pressed herself closer against the man who held her.

He kissed her until the scented carriage with its fragrant flowers seemed to move dizzily round her.

Then when she wanted him to kiss her and go on kissing her he set her free.

'*Au revoir, ma Princesse,*' he said very softly.

Swiftly, and yet so softly that she could hardly hear him go, he left her and she was alone in the carriage with only the flowers and the beating of her heart.

# CHAPTER FOUR

As the train moved slowly down from the pass towards the valley Zenka thought she had never seen anything so beautiful.

The mountains which surrounded Karanya were silhouetted against the blue sky, some of their peaks still covered with the winter snows.

But the sun-shine was brilliant and as the train descended there were alpine plateaux covered with a profusion of brilliant flowers.

On the little stations they passed and on the balconies of the white wooden houses with their sloping roofs there were also flowers of every colour.

Zenka thought it so lovely and so reminiscent of Vajda that she felt the tears come into her eyes, and it was hard to see the children waiting by the line to wave from the moment

143

the train came into sight.

She had woken after a deep sleep with a feeling of happiness that she had not known since she had first been told that she was to marry King Miklos.

Then she told herself she should feel embarrassed and ashamed of her behaviour of the night before.

How could she ever have imagined, she asked herself, that she would talk intimately with a thief in the darkness and then allow him to kiss her?

She should be appalled at the immodesty of such behaviour, but instead she asked herself defiantly what did it matter?

'Who am I keeping myself for?' she questioned.

She had been brought up to believe that her first kiss should be for the man she loved, the man who would be her husband.

But when she had talked of such things and believed them, she was not to know that her husband would be King Miklos and that her marriage would not be one of love but on her part one of hatred.

She had a feeling that although he would never know it she had scored off the King and taken from him something he would think was his by right.

'Not that I have any intention of letting him kiss me,' Zenka said to herself.

She had been planning ever since she left England what her attitude would be towards the King.

Now because the thief had in some way inspired her with a new courage, the plan that had been forming hazily in her mind suddenly became clear, like a jig-saw puzzle falling into place so that she knew exactly what she would do.

She did not wish to think about it at this moment but instead concentrated on the country that was to be her future home, and which despite its King she thought she would love because it reminded her of Vajda.

The train proceeded very slowly and it was nearly mid-day when finally Vitza was in sight.

The Capital was built in the very centre of the valley and at first sight its white houses, round-topped Mosques and high Minarets gave it a fairy-like appearance.

But for Zenka the enchantment of what she had seen had now gone, and now that the moment was upon her when she would meet the King of Karanya she felt the fear that she had acknowledged last night creeping back.

She went to her bed-room to put on her bonnet and Fanni had ready her long kid-gloves.

Zenka glanced at herself in the mirror and tried to think that her new gown was an armour with which she would go into battle.

She had chosen it because she thought it was how the people of Karanya would expect their Queen to look on arrival.

It was white, decorated with a blue sash which echoed the colour of the alpine flower. Narrow ribbons of the same colour were threaded through the frills which formed a

146

bustle at the back and there were blue ribbons at her throat and her wrists, and which also tied her bonnet under her chin.

It made her look young and very lovely, and yet the gown itself had a sophistication and a chic which proclaimed that the design had come from Paris.

'You look very beautiful, Your Royal Highness,' Fanni murmured. 'My people will be very proud that they have such a beautiful Queen.'

Zenka wondered what the King would think, then told herself that he was used to sophisticated women and doubtless his mistress, like Nita Loplakovoff, would look exotic and perhaps seductive in a manner that she could not emulate.

Then she tossed her head and told herself it did not matter in the least what he thought as long as he did not assume she was the crushed, submissive wife whom he would expect Queen Victoria to send him.

The train was moving into the station and now there was a knock at the door to tell her the rest of the party was already waiting in the Drawing-Room.

It had been arranged that the King should step into the train on its arrival and be introduced to his future bride before they faced the crowds outside.

At the very last moment Zenka came from her bed-room and saw by the expression on the Ambassador's face that he was anxious that she should make a good impression immediately on her arrival.

Her Godfather gave her a reassuring smile, while the Duchess was looking petulant as if already she was seeking to find fault with the arrangements.

It was, Zenka knew, because she was growing more and more jealous that she was not the centre of attraction and that she had to take second place to her husband's Ward.

'It is a pity she cannot marry the King instead of me!' Zenka thought.

Then because she knew it would annoy the Duchess she slipped her hand into her Godfather's saying:

'I know you will understand that this is rather embarrassing and makes me feel shy.'

His fingers pressed hers and he said:

'The introduction will soon be over. Then I am sure you will enjoy seeing your new Capital and realise how enthusiastically the people are ready to welcome you.'

Zenka forced herself to smile at him, knowing that he was trying to be reassuring.

The train came to a standstill and the Ambassador and the Secretary for Foreign Affairs hurried to the doorway so that they could step out and greet the King who would be waiting on the platform.

There was the sound of the Guard of Honour coming to attention, then voices speaking respectfully and a moment later the King came into the carriage.

For a moment Zenka really felt as shy and embarrassed as she was pretending to be.

Then as she swept down in curtsey with her eyes lowered she realised the King was standing in front of her and her gloved hand was in his.

'May I welcome you Your Royal Highness to Karanya,' he said speaking English. 'It is a very happy day for my country and for me in particular and I hope with all my heart that we can make you happy too.'

It was, Zenka thought scornfully, a well-rehearsed speech and as she rose from her curtsey she replied:

'I thank Your Majesty.'

It had been suggested that she should say a great deal more but she had refused. Now she spoke in what she hoped was a cold, indifferent voice and she deliberately did not raise her eyes to look at him.

The Ambassador was at the King's side.

'May I, Your Majesty, present the Duke of Stirling?'

'I am delighted to meet Your Grace,' the King said, 'and it is extremely kind of you to accompany your Ward to my country.'

'May I, Your Majesty, present the Duchess of Stirling?'

The Duchess embarked on a gushing, flattering eulogy which Zenka knew she should have made herself, and now for the first time she peeped from under her eye-lashes at the King.

He was certainly not as deformed as Wilhelmina had made out, in fact he was much taller than she had expected and very broad-shouldered; or perhaps it was the fringed gold epaulettes which made his shoulders seem almost exaggeratedly broad compared to the slimness of his waist and the narrowness of his hips.

Then she looked at his face and saw that while the right side was untouched the left side had a heavy scar from his forehead to the end of his eye-brow and another scar beneath it on his cheek.

She realised that without such scars he would have been good-looking, or perhaps striking was the right word.

He had the clear-cut features which had been characteristic of her father, a pronounced nose, a broad square forehead, deep-set dark eyes and a firm mouth.

But the scars, which were now healed but must have been extremely predominant when they were first made, gave him a raffish, strange look.

It made Zenka feel that he resembled one of the pirate chiefs who once roamed the Mediterranean and made the Barbary Coast an inferno for the Christians they took prisoner.

'He looks like a pirate...or should it be a bandit?' she asked herself.

She thought scornfully that perhaps he was descended from the bandit bands who haunted the mountains in this part of the world and were known for their savagery.

She remembered the Pallikaras who were legendary mercenaries and cut-throats and lived in the Albanian mountains in strongholds from which no-one could dislodge them.

Their leaders were tall, handsome and seductive and at the same time, ferocious and barbaric.

They swaggered about, heavily moustachioed, in crimson and gold embroidery bristling with pistols and yataghans.

'That is who he is like,' she decided.

Watching him as he greeted the other members of the party she told herself that, even though he was not as revolting to look at as Wilhelmina had suggested, she perhaps hated him even more because she now found no reason to feel sorry for him.

She suspected that the scars on his forehead and cheek were made in a duel by some irate husband who had caught him making love to his wife.

'It is a pity he did not kill him!' Zenka thought vindictively.

Then as the King turned towards her once again she quickly lowered her eyes, hoping that for the moment he would think her young and shy and would not realise how much she hated him.

'Are you ready to leave?' the King asked. 'It is arranged that we should drive through the city to the Palace and my people are very eager to welcome you.'

Zenka did not answer, she merely inclined her head and they moved towards the entrance.

As they did so she wondered what the King would think if she showed him the exact spot where she had stood last night and allowed herself to be kissed by a French thief.

He would doubtless be scandalised and at the same time incensed that his sentries had not taken proper care of her, and she knew she could not tell him because it would get them into trouble.

'Perhaps one day I will taunt him with it,' she told herself and felt it was another weapon with which she could fight him.

He helped her down onto the platform and now the crowds who were waiting behind the barrier on the station burst into loud cheers.

As they moved along a red carpet which led them to the entrance Zenka saw an arch made of palm-leaves and flowers with the inscription: *'Welcome to the English Princess!'*

That, combined with the profusion of

Union Jacks, told her that the King and his countrymen were emphasising the fact that she was half-English and forgetting that she was in fact Hungarian according to her father's nationality.

It lit the fires of anger that were already smouldering within her to think that her father should be set aside and her Hungarian blood dismissed as unimportant.

She waited until they were seated in the carriage with the King beside her and the Duke and the Prime Minister with their backs to the horses before she mentioned the subject.

The Duchess was following in the next carriage with the Secretary of State for Foreign Affairs, the British Ambassador to Karanya and the Ambassador of Karanya who had travelled with them in the ship.

There was one moment before the carriage pulled out of the station-yard onto the main road when Zenka was able to lean forward and say to the man opposite her:

'I am surprised, Prime Minister, to see

that I am acclaimed as an *English Princess*. You must have forgotten that I am in fact Hungarian.'

As she expected the Prime Minister looked uncomfortable.

'Hungary, Your Royal Highness, is now united with Austria,' he replied, 'and the Austrians are being somewhat difficult at the moment. In fact I will be frank and say they are very unpopular in Karanya.'

'The Hungarians have no liking for the Austrians either,' Zenka replied, 'but I should be grateful if you would remember that I am my father's daughter and very proud of the fact.'

She did not look at the King as she spoke but knew he was attentive to what she had said.

Then they were out on the main road and the deafening cheers made it impossible for her to be heard even if she had wished to say anything further.

All along the route there were children waving Union Jacks, the red, white and blue mingling with the gold and green of the Karanyan flags.

They passed under a number of triumphal arches and bunches of flowers were thrown into their carriage, although many fell on the roadway to be trampled under the feet of the horses drawing the carriages or of Cavalry escorting them.

It was all very similar to what Zenka had recently seen in London at the Queen's Golden Jubilee.

But however *blasé* she might try to be, she could not ignore the beauty of the mountains in the distance, the golden glitter of the sun and the attractiveness of the crowds themselves.

She had expected the women to look pretty and that they would be wearing costumes very much the same as those worn by the peasants in every Balkan country.

The full red or blue skirts seemed however to be fashioned in even more brilliant colours than she remembered, the white blouses more skilfully embroidered and the head-dresses with their colourful ribbons and flowers to be undeniably attractive.

In the crowd too there were men wearing the lambs-wool or catskin caps of those who lived amongst the mountains, while others wore wide sombreros ornamented with ribbons or small wool caps embroidered in the colours of the alpine flowers.

It was as if the rainbow had fallen out of the sky and spilled itself over the people who cheered her, and for a moment Zenka forgot the King and waved happily to those she passed with the spontaneous enjoyment of a child.

Then she saw the Palace, an enormous white building built on a slope a little above the town and having a rather austere look which brought back her fears.

It was noble and splendid, but to Zenka it was a Palace, and she knew only too well that Palaces meant heavy protocol, organised duties and usually a chilly atmosphere.

Now that the noise from the crowd was fading and the front of the Palace was empty except for a Guard of Honour and three fountains, it was possible to hear one's own voice.

'A demonstration of great sincerity, Your Royal Highness,' the Prime Minister was saying. 'The people of Karanya have taken you to their hearts.'

'That is very gratifying,' Zenka said with just a touch of sarcasm in her voice, 'but it is, I feel, the Union Jack they are saluting.'

As she spoke she glanced at the King for the first time since they left the station and had to admit that in his plumed hat with the blue ribbon crossing the breast of his white tunic he looked very magnificent.

'He is a bandit,' she thought with a twist of her lips and put her hand in his so that he could lead her up the steps of the Palace.

Inside it was more spacious than she had expected. There were life-size marble statues in a hall where exquisite plaster-work was reflected in huge mirrors which also reflected and re-reflected herself and the King.

There was a floor of tessellated marble,

159

another of quartz, and a third of lapis-lazuli before they reached an enormous Ball-Room which was filled with all the noble and important personages of Karanya.

The King led her to a dais on which stood two carved and gilded thrones, and standing under a canopy of red silk embroidered with the Royal coat-of-arms they began to receive those who were to be presented.

Long before the seemingly endless line of people had filed past Zenka had ceased to register anything of the faces which swam in front of her as they repeated the same congratulatory sentences over and over again like a monotonous note of music.

'Thank you.' 'It is very kind of you.' 'I am most grateful,' she repeated in Karanyan until she thought she would say them in her sleep.

Then at last there were no more presentations and some one put a glass of champagne in her hand which she sipped thankfully.

'I am most impressed and appreciative that

you should speak our language so well,' the King remarked.

'It is not unlike Hungarian,' Zenka replied coldly. 'In fact a great number of the words are the same.'

'I am aware of that, but I still did not expect you to be so fluent.'

Zenka knew he was trying to be pleasant, but the mere fact that he was congratulating her made her feel as if her hackles were rising almost like those of an angry fox-terrier.

How dare he assume, she thought to herself, that a Hungarian would not be able to speak the language of an adjacent country; how dare he be surprised at her intelligence?

She deliberately turned aside to speak to the British Ambassador, an elderly, rather pompous man who was, she thought, basking in the success of having provided a so-called "English" Princess like a rabbit out of a hat.

'Surely, Your Excellency, the Hungarian Ambassador is here?' she asked. 'I should like to meet him.'

'He was not invited, Ma'am.'

'Not invited?' Zenka asked. 'How astonishing!'

'Austria, and that includes Hungary, has been making trouble on the borders of Karanya and one of the reasons why you are so very welcome is because Your Royal Highness brings the assurance that Great Britain will now support our independence.'

'That of course is the one and only reason I am here,' Zenka said.

'Whatever it might be, the Karanyans welcome you, Ma'am, with open arms.'

'I see that I shall have to make it very clear to them, and of course to you, that I am in fact Hungarian,' Zenka said and saw the expression of consternation on his face.

With a smile she moved away, then found she was expected to sit on the throne next to the King while the Mayor of Karanya made an address of welcome on behalf of the city.

It was a long, rather rambling speech, but one thing he said struck Zenka almost as if it was written on the walls in letters of fire.

'For two hundred years, Your Majesty,' the Mayor read from a scroll in his hands, 'your illustrious ancestors have ruled over our country and brought us both justice and peace. On this happy occasion when you have brought us a beautiful English Princess to be your Queen you have also brought us hope for the future.

'It is through the succession of the Dynasty that we shall preserve our independence and security, and as we look to you, Sire, to lead us into an era of prosperity we look also to the future when your sons and grandsons will do the same for our children.'

'The succession!' the words seemed to burn themselves into Zenka's mind.

So she was not wanted only because she was British but because she would be a "breeding machine" for the future Kings of Karanya!

She supposed that it should have struck her before that this would be expected of her.

But she had been so taken up with the thought that the arranged marriage was simply and solely to preserve the balance of power that she had forgotten that as the King's wife he would expect her to give him sons to bear his name.

She was so angry at suddenly realising this that she could think of nothing else and was almost brusque in her replies to those who spoke to her when the speeches were over.

Fortunately it was time for luncheon. In fact Zenka thought, feeling very hungry, that it was long past the time when they should have sat down to a meal.

The same had happened at the Queen's Jubilee when luncheon was not served until three o'clock in the gold and white Dining-Room which overlooked an artificial lake at the back of the Palace.

Through the window Zenka could see exquisitely laid out gardens, and the water gleaming in the sun-shine made her long to dispense with the long-drawn-out meal and many more long-drawn-out speeches.

The King's speech was short and witty, but though he paid her extravagant compliments she was still too angry to listen.

Only when at last it was all over and she withdrew with the Duchess followed by her Ladies-in-waiting to what she was told were the "Queen's Apartments", did she feel as if she had been dragged through a mangle.

She was limp with exhaustion and her own surging feelings of anger and resentment.

'You were not looking very pleasant at luncheon,' the Duchess remarked.

Zenka knew she was pleased at being able to find fault.

'I had nothing to be pleased about.'

'I cannot think why not,' the Duchess snapped. 'Look at this Palace! Have you ever seen anything more magnificent? It makes Buckingham Palace and Windsor Castle look shabby and out of date.'

Zenka did not answer.

She was not going to admit that she was in fact thrilled by the huge bed-room they had just entered.

It was the loveliest room she had ever seen.

There were carvings of cupids, doves and butterflies everywhere, and the bed, which must have been made in the 18th century, was so exquisite that it was like something from a fairy-tale.

The hangings were of soft blue, the colour of a sky in summer, and the carpet which was an Aubousson was a riot of flowers and blue-ribbons.

The windows overlooked the gardens and just for a moment Zenka longed to tell the truth and say she could not imagine anything lovelier or more imaginative.

Then she remembered who it belonged to and who had undoubtedly planned it.

'There is even a bath-room next door,' the Duchess was saying. 'Goodness, but you are a lucky girl! If you are not happy here, you would not be happy anywhere.'

Zenka did not reply. She was untying the ribbons on her bonnet and running her fingers through her red hair.

'I am tired and I would like to rest,' she said.

'And I certainly want to do the same,' the Duchess retorted sharply. 'I suppose you have heard that the King with the greatest consideration has arranged that we shall dine *en famille* this evening so that you will not be tired to-morrow for your wedding.'

'How very thoughtful of him,' Zenka forced herself to say, but she did not sound as if she was pleased.

Then to her relief she was left alone except for Fanni, who came to help her undress.

She was actually so tired, through having so little sleep the night before and because she was agitated and upset within herself, that she did not get up for dinner.

What was the point, she wondered, of upsetting herself still further by listening to the spiteful remarks of the Duchess when she might as well stay in bed?

Although she refused to admit it to herself the beautiful room had a soothing effect on her.

She found it hard to feel as angry as she had been when she lay in the magnificent bed under a canopy of rampant cupids and looked out onto the sunshine turning the lake into a sea of gold.

Fanni looked after her as if she was a child, and after the Duke and Duchess had come to say good night to her she fell asleep while she was thinking not of her King and her hatred for him but of the thief.

He had held her captive with his lips and aroused strange sensations she had never known before which were as lovely and wonderful as the room in which she was sleeping.

★ ★ ★ ★

'It is a beautiful day, Your Royal Highness,' Fanni said when she called Zenka the following morning and added as she pulled back the curtains: 'The crowds have been up all night in order to get a good place to see you

168

when you drive to the Cathedral.'

'My Wedding Day!' Zenka thought to herself and longed to shut her eyes, turn over and go back to sleep again.

Could it really be now, the day she had dreaded, the moment when she must become the wife of a man she hated? A man who had married her because of her British Royal blood and intended that she should produce his children without love.

Zenka wanted to cry out that they would be as deformed as their father, but she could not in all honesty say that the King was as deformed as she had expected.

His scars certainly made one side of his face look very strange, but otherwise he moved athletically with no sign of a limp which Wilhelmina had told her to expect, and she supposed that most women would find him attractive.

When later she drove beside the Duke towards the Cathedral she told herself that she felt as cold and as hard as a stone.

She was no longer tremulous with anger

and her fears seemed to have left her.

She held herself proudly and told herself that now the fight with the man about to become her husband was to begin she would make quite certain of being the victor.

'Your reception is very gratifying, my dear,' the Duke said as the cheers were almost deafening and the flowers bestrewed the road every yard of the way.

With her face covered by the veil and wearing on her head a diamond tiara, Zenka did not wave because she knew it was not expected of her.

She had been fussed over by the Mistress of the Robes and the other ladies of the Court, who believed it was their right to be present when she put on her veil and the jewels they brought to her bed-room.

There was a necklace which equalled the one that had encircled the long, swan-like neck of the Princess of Wales, and she was informed that the tiara she would wear as she drove to the Cathedral would be changed during the service.

The King would crown her as his Queen and it was this crown she would wear on the return journey to the Palace.

There were bracelets for her wrists and a diamond corsage to ornament the front of her tightly fitting gown which revealed the curves of her breasts and the tininess of her waist.

Because she was having no bridesmaids her gown had a train built into it. Falling from the bustle it swept out behind like a spray of diamonds and yet was so light that she needed no pages to carry it.

By the time she was dressed Zenka somehow felt disembodied and aloof from everything that was happening to her.

The cheers of the crowds, the clutter of the Cavalry escorting her carriage, the flowers that paved the way, were all like something that was happening in a dream.

'I am very proud of you,' the Duke said just before they arrived at the Cathedral. 'I know this is something of an ordeal, but you

171

are carrying it off with flying colours, and I know your father, if he was here, would say the same.'

Just for a moment his words seemed to break through the granite wall behind which Zenka had incarcerated herself, and she felt the tears prick her eyes.

Then the trumpeters were sounding a fanfare and she stepped out at the West Door of the Cathedral to walk up the aisle on the Duke's arm to where the King was waiting for her at the Chancel steps.

She felt him stand beside her and told herself the Marriage Service in which she was taking part was a farce.

A marriage was wrong and wicked unless two people loved each other, and that was something that would never happen where she was concerned.

She deliberately shut her eyes to the words that were being said and only when she knew that the Archbishop was waiting for her to say: 'I will,' did she realise that her thoughts had been far away.

She felt the King take her hand in his and put the ring on her finger. Then they were moving up the altar steps and Zenka began to pray for courage. It was a cry that came from her very heart.

'Please God, make me brave. Make me fight for what I believe to be right as my ancestors fought.'

She repeated the words a dozen times, not listening to the Archbishop's address.

Then while she remained kneeling the King took the Queen's crown from the Archbishop and the Mistress of the Robes lifted the diamond tiara from Zenka's head.

The King placed the crown on Zenka's head saying:

'I crown you Queen of Karanya, and may you bring our people peace and happiness.'

He helped her rise and turned her round to face the congregation.

As he did so everyone in the Cathedral shouted: 'Long life to the Queen!'

The sound of their voices was very moving

and once again Zenka felt the tears prick her eyes.

She and the King knelt in front of the Archbishop and he blessed them both. Then the music of the organ swelled out as they walked slowly down the aisle.

The ladies swept to the ground in deep curtsies as they passed, and the men bowed their heads.

It had all been very well organised and the whole ceremony had gone off without a hitch, but Zenka knew there were a great many more ceremonies to be endured before the wedding-day was over.

Now she drove back to the Palace at the King's side but felt there was no reason to speak to him or even to look at him.

She waved and bowed to the people on her side of the gold coach in which they travelled and he did the same on his side.

The noise of the crowd was deafening and the white horses which drew them, not unlike those which had carried Queen Victoria to Westminster Abbey, moved very slowly.

It took a long time to reach the Palace and Zenka's arm was aching and her face felt stiff from smiling, before they turned in at the gold tipped gates as they drove into the court-yard of the Palace, and the King leant back and said:

'Well, thank goodness we never need be married again.'

Zenka turned her face towards him for the first time.

'I am only so surprised that you have not been married before,' she said.

'It is something I have managed to avoid up till now,' he replied.

She thought his answer was almost astonishing and very different from the compliments he had paid her in public.

But there was no time for conversation; for the footmen in their white wigs were opening the doors of the carriage and officials of the Palace who had returned from the Cathedral by a different and quicker route led them to the Ball-Room.

Once again there was the long presentation

of people to be received, toasts to be drunk and an enormous six-feet-high wedding-cake to be cut.

It was all so familiar and so like the other Royal weddings that Zenka had attended at one time or another, that she almost felt as if she herself had been married many times before.

Then at last when it seemed the day would never end it was over, and she went to her bed-room feeling the crown on her head was weighing her down. It had grown heavier hour by hour.

After the Reception was finished she had not been allowed to escape as she had expected. Instead there had been a large dinner-party for the Duke and Duchess who were to depart so early the next morning that Zenka was to say good-bye to them that night.

It might have been a departure from what was usually expected from a bride and groom, but because she had been travelling for so long the King had decided they would not leave for their honeymoon until the end of the week.

'I am taking you to my Castle in the mountains,' he said. 'Which I think you will enjoy. It is quite a long journey, so I have arranged, unless you have other ideas, that we should stay here at the Palace for the next three days.'

'I have no other ideas,' Zenka replied.

She was amused at his choice of the Castle for their honeymoon; for that was where she had heard the orgies took place and she wondered what he would think if she asked him what happened at them.

It would certainly be a very different visit from those he had paid to the Castle in the past, she told herself.

Zenka had said good-bye to her Godfather, and as she did she wondered what he would say if she should ask to return to England with him.

Then she told herself that if she even showed emotion in parting from him, Duchess Kathleen doubtless would be pleased about it.

With an effort she bit back the words she wanted to say and merely kissed him good-bye.

'You will write and tell me what is happening in Scotland?'

'Of course,' he answered, 'and I shall want to hear what is happening in Karanya.'

They smiled at each other and she had the feeling that he understood what she was feeling but had no words with which to comfort her.

The Duchess kissed her perfunctorily on the cheek.

'I hope you enjoy being so grand, Zenka,' she said with the usual sharp note in her voice. 'At least I can congratulate myself that in the new gowns I chose you will look a Queen!'

The implication that Zenka would not behave like one was very obvious.

'Good-bye,' Zenka said and deliberately refrained from making some sarcastic remark which the Duchess would only find amusing.

In her bed-room Zenka took the crown

from her head and handed it to the Mistress of the Robes who was waiting to convey it and the other jewels she had worn to a place of safety.

'Good-night, Ma'am,' she said as carrying the jewels in her hand she curtsied at the door. 'May I wish you once again every happiness.'

There was a smile on her lips and an innuendo in her voice which Zenka resented because she knew it was what she should expect on her bridal night.

She knew exactly what the Mistress of the Robes was thinking and she was perhaps envying her too, because Zenka was sure that like all the other women in the Court she thought the King was irresistibly attractive.

She had noticed the way they fawned on him when he spoke to them, and she saw too the looks they gave him while he was sitting beside her at luncheon.

Their eyes told him quite boldly how much they would like to change places with his wife.

'I wonder how many of them he has made love to,' Zenka thought scornfully.

Fanni helped her off with her gown and brought her one of the exquisite nightgowns that she and the Duchess had purchased in London.

There was an even more elaborate lace wrap which had cost as much as an evening-gown. It billowed out round her feet in a dozen lace frills, and her red hair falling over her shoulders covered the frills which trimm-ed the neck.

'Is Your Majesty not going to get into bed?' Fanni asked as Zenka put it on.

'Not for the moment,' Zenka replied, 'and you can leave me now, Fanni.'

'Yes, of course, Your Majesty. Shall I ex-tinguish some of the lights?'

'No, leave them.'

'Then good-night, Your Majesty. May God bless you and may you have a quiet and peaceful night.'

Zenka waited for the door to shut behind Fanni. Then she opened her glove-box which she herself unpacked from her dressing-case and put in a drawer.

It was locked and she had a little key which opened it. Inside lying on top of her gloves was the pistol which the Duke had given her after she had been with him to the shooting-school.

She took it out, saw that it was loaded and looked down at it with a smile on her lips.

Last night she had not had it ready to hand when she had needed it, and she remembered how the thief had said that ladies usually did not walk about in their nightgowns with a pistol in their hand.

He was wrong. To-night she would not be caught without a pistol in her hand.

She sat down on the stool in front of the dressing-table with her back to the mirror, her eyes on a communicating door which led into the King's apartments.

She wondered if this beautiful room, which although it had been re-decorated had obviously been the Queen's room for many

181

generations, had ever known a bride like herself.

She told herself scathingly that the Kings in the past had married subservient, frightened little women whom they bullied into obedience.

But King Miklos was going to have a surprise.

It seemed to Zenka that she waited for a long time. Then as she heard a step outside the door and the handle turned she rose to her feet.

She held the pistol down at her side so that it was hidden against the flowing folds of her white robe, as the King came into the room.

He was wearing a dark red robe which reached to the ground, and there was a scarf around his neck. Somehow he contrived to look as if he was fully dressed and for a moment Zenka wished that she had kept on her evening gown.

He shut the door behind him and stood for a moment looking at her.

She was angry that he should see her with

her hair loose over her shoulders wearing only a nightgown and a satin robe.

Because her heart was beating unaccountably loud she said, and her voice seemed to ring out:

'Why are you...here?'

'I should have thought that was obvious,' the King replied.

He would have moved towards her, but Zenka put up her pistol and levelled it at him.

'If you think you are welcome in my bedroom you are very much mistaken!' she said.

The King stood still and she went on:

'I have been forced to marry you because you need a so-called British Princess to bolster up your independence, and prevent you being overrun by your neighbours. If you think that entitles you to treat me as if I was your mistress you are very much mistaken!'

'I will treat you as my wife, which is what you are,' the King answered.

'To make sure of the succession?'

'It is usually the result of a marriage between a man and a woman.'

'But ours is not a usual marriage,' Zenka said. 'You do not want me, you want what I represent. In which case you can go to bed with the Union Jack.'

It was rude, but she was angry.

She felt as if her eyes blazed at him and the words came tumbling from her lips because she was beginning to burn with the flames of resentment.

'Is that how you feel?' the King asked.

'I can make if plainer if you wish,' Zenka said. 'You disgust me and I hate you! If you come near me or touch me I will shoot you!'

She gave a little laugh of defiance.

'I will not kill you. I am not as foolish as that. I have no wish to be branded as a murderer, but I will shoot you in the arm and that should enable me to be free of your advances for some weeks at any rate.'

She was almost spitting the words at him. Then to her astonishment he began to laugh. He threw back his head and his laughter seemed to echo round the room and fill it.

'Magnificent!' he said. 'Quite magnificent! My dear girl, if you had no wish to marry me, has it never occurred to you that I feel exactly the same?'

Zenka's eyes widened to fill her whole face.

'You mean...you did not...wish to marry me.'

'Of course not!' the King answered. 'Good heavens, do you really imagine that if I had a choice I should want, at my age, a wife who is little more than an unfledged school-girl, twelve years younger than myself, who knows nothing of the world and certainly nothing of the things that I find amusing.'

Zenka could only stare at him and now her hand with the revolver dropped to her side.

'I can see that someone has been filling your head with a lot of ridiculous ideas,' the King went on. 'Perhaps the Ambassador even said I was in love with you. Well, quite frankly the sooner we have a sensible talk about all this the better! Suppose we sit down?'

He made a gesture with his hand towards the satin sofa which stood in front of the flower-filled fireplace.

Almost as if she was sleep-walking Zenka moved towards it and sat down on the edge of the sofa, while the King seated himself in an arm-chair and leaned back at his ease.

'You are very young,' he said in a condescending tone, 'but I suppose you were far too frightened of the Queen Empress to tell her you had no wish to marry me.'

'I did not get the...chance,' Zenka replied. 'The Duke, as my Guardian, agreed to her suggestion. Then everything was arranged without my having a say...in it.'

'You poor child! It was grossly unfair,' the King said. 'I have fought for a year against having to take an English bride to protect Karanya, until finally there was nothing more I could do to prevent it.'

'Why?' Zenka asked.

'You know the answer to that,' the King

replied. 'Austria was determined to annex us, and the only thing that stood in her way was that Turkey had the same idea.'

He gave a short laugh.

'Great Britain was our only life-belt.'

'I thought I was a parcel tied up with the Union Jack,' Zenka said. 'I had not thought of being a life-belt.'

'You can take your choice,' the King answered casually. 'They both mean the same thing.'

He looked at her and she thought he was somehow critical. Then he said:

'We are both in the same boat and therefore we might as well make the most of it.'

Zenka did not reply and he rose to his feet.

'I can re-assure you by telling you there is no need for you to use your pop-gun,' he said. 'It will cause a great deal of comment if we do not appear in public together, but your private life is of course your own.'

'Thank...you.'

Zenka did not sound as grateful, she

thought, as she ought to have done, but instead curiously deflated.

It was one thing to fight the King with fire, courage and spirit, but quite another to fight a battle that was unnecessary.

'Well, I hope you sleep well,' the King said, 'and that you are pleased with your room. I designed it a long time ago, and always hoped that whoever slept in it would appreciate the furnishings and of course the bed.'

'You say you designed it a long time ago,' Zenka said.

'Perhaps that is exaggerating,' he replied. 'It is only a year, but it seems longer.'

'It is very beautiful.'

'I am glad you think so, I suppose I always imagined that my Queen would be dark-haired, so perhaps there is rather too much pink in the carpet.'

'I like it...as it is.'

'Then we will leave it,' the King said. 'Good-night, Zenka.'

He rose and walked across the room and

as he reached the door he said:

'By the way, I think we might go to the theatre to-morrow evening. Nita Loplakovoff is dancing, and if you have never seen her I can assure you she is one of the most outstanding Ballerinas in the world to-day.'

He opened the door and left without waiting for a reply.

Zenka sat where he had left her.

She sat for a long time looking at the pistol she held in her lap.

# CHAPTER FIVE

Driving through the streets beside the King, Zenka looked at the decorations with interest.

Yesterday because of the vast crowds and her own desperate feelings she had been unable to see them or notice them very closely when she drove to the Cathedral and when she drove back.

But to-day with the sunshine pouring over the city it looked very attractive with flags and arches of flowers, blending in with the colourful clothes of the people.

Because they were not escorted by soldiers and the King was driving a Cabriole many of the people did not recognise them and Zenka was able to look at the different types of Karanyans moving about the streets and to admire the women.

190

Many of them were very beautiful and the men had that free, proud carriage which reminded her of the men in Vajda.

She had slept late and when she woke she was informed by Fanni that there was a luncheon-party at which she was expected to be present.

She had lain awake for a long time after the King had left her, not certain of her own feelings.

They should have been feelings of relief, and yet something perverse and rebellious within her resented the fact that the King had won a bloodless victory when she had least expected it.

How could she have known? How could she have guessed for one moment what his feelings would be? And while she had tried to tell herself it was exactly what she had wished for she knew in her heart that she wanted to go on fighting him.

It seemed ridiculous now that she had ever imagined for a moment that the King would not feel just as she did about their arranged marriage, and she thought if nothing else it would certainly teach her that she was not so attractive that no man could resist her.

One thing that was quite obvious, she thought: the King was quite prepared to treat the marriage as a business arrangement and avoid anything personal or intimate.

When she appeared in the Salon where she was told they were to meet before luncheon, he greeted her with courtesy, raising her hand perfunctorily to his lips. Then he presented the guests to her.

It was all very informal and she knew that in most Palaces the guests would have been obliged to arrive first and stand stiffly in a row before they were presented by a aide-de-camp to the King and Queen.

Instead of which the King moved about chatting to everybody, making them laugh, and luncheon was in fact a relaxing and amusing meal.

It was not long-drawn-out and the few courses there were were original and well cooked.

When the guests departed the King said:

'I promised, and I hope it will not bore you, that we would visit our new Zoo this afternoon. It is something of which Vitza is very proud.'

'I would like it very much,' Zenka answered.

She hurried upstairs to put on a bonnet which matched her gown of pale green. It made her look like a nymph of spring, and carrying a small sun-shade she went downstairs to find the King intended to drive her himself in a new Cabriole which he told her had been copied from those which were all the rage in Paris.

He was looking very much less formal than he had yesterday in his uniform.

Now he was arrayed conventionally in clothes that any gentleman anywhere in the world might have worn, with a top-hat on the side of his dark head.

He drove well, and since there was not very much traffic on the outskirts of the city he let his horses move at a sharp pace along

193

the roads bordered with flowering trees.

'Vitza is very pretty,' Zenka said after a while, feeling it was rude not to speak.

'Not half as pretty as my Castle at Tisza,' the King replied, 'and I have some horses there which I hope you will enjoy riding.'

Zenka's eyes lit up.

'I cannot tell you how much I have missed the horses I used to ride at home in Vajda,' she said. 'My father and I would gallop for miles over the Steppes and no horse I have ridden in England or Scotland has ever been their equal.'

'I can understand that,' the King said, 'and I admire a woman who can ride well.'

There was a slightly reminiscent note in his voice which made Zenka think he was remembering the women he had admired, but she found herself thinking with satisfaction that everyone who had ever seen her on a horse had told her that she was an outstanding rider.

'I think I had forgotten that you ever lived in Vajda,' he went on, 'because I was wondering if my horses would be too spirited and too strong for you.'

'That is an insult!' Zenka exclaimed.

'I shall be delighted to have you prove me wrong,' the King replied.

She thought he did not sound as if he was certain she would do so, and she told herself determinedly that sooner or later she would make him acknowledge how good a horse-woman she was.

The new Zoo was about two miles outside the town and far more attractive to look at than any Zoo Zenka had ever seen before.

The animals were in large open spaces in which they could move about freely and everything had been done to make it appear as if they were in their natural surroundings.

There were lions, tigers and leopards all lying under shady trees. There were also giraffes and kangaroos and a large number of bears.

'These of course are natural to Karanya,' the King explained to Zenka.

'I am afraid, Your Majesty,' the Keeper

195

said, 'that we find it very difficult not to acquire more bears than we actually require. The peasants capture the cubs in the mountains and bring them to us hoping we will pay them for their trouble.'

He smiled as he added:

'The Tziganes when their dancing animals breed find it tiresome to travel with the cubs as well.'

Zenka picked up a small cub that looked like a small ball of fur.

'They are so sweet,' she said, 'I would like to keep one with me for a pet.'

'I am afraid you would find him very destructive,' the King answered, 'and I really cannot afford to have him tear your bedroom to pieces when it has only recently been completed.'

'Perhaps he would prove to be a good watch-dog,' Zenka suggested.

She spoke without it having any particular meaning, just making conversation, but the King answered in a voice that only she could hear:

'I have assured you there is no need for one.'

She could not meet his eyes and blushed.

It was the first reference he had made to her behaviour last night and now she felt embarrassed by it.

It seemed in retrospect somehow theatrical and melodramatic, and yet she had been sure when she had contrived to make the Duke give her a pistol in London that she would find it necessary to keep the King from touching her.

It was obvious from the way he talked to the Keepers at the Zoo that he knew a great deal about animals.

She noticed that those he handled licked his hand and seemed to trust him with that unfailing instinct of wild creatures who know who they can trust and who they cannot.

They looked at the snakes in the small snake-house combined with Aquarium that had been built in the centre of the Zoo and Zenka shivered.

'I hate snakes!' she said.

'Then they will hate you,' the King answered. 'I have seen men in India who, because they will not take life and love everything that breathes, can handle the most poisonous snakes without fear and without ever being in danger of being bitten.'

'You have been to India?' Zenka asked with interest. 'It is a country I have always longed to visit.'

'I have travelled to a great many places in the world,' the King answered, 'but I think India is one of those I love the best.'

'I hope you will tell me about it,' Zenka said.

'Perhaps sometime,' the King replied, 'when we have nothing better to do.'

He spoke indifferently and moved away to look at some tropical fish and Zenka felt snubbed.

She had a sudden feeling of loneliness; of being unwanted; and to hide her feelings as soon as they emerged from the snake-house she picked up another of the baby bears and cuddled it in her arms.

As she did so she thought perhaps it would be rather wonderful to have a child of her own. At least a baby would prevent her from feeling unwanted.

Then as she saw the King moving away surrounded by the officials talking to him eagerly, she told herself that she had to be self-sufficient and that if her pride was wavering it was only because she was tired.

She followed the King and there were a great many other things to see.

They saw plans for an extension of the Zoo, but one of the officials said it might be a long time before it was put into action because they had run out of money.

'I think it would be a good idea,' the King said, 'until we can afford the more exotic animals from overseas, to have some of our own wild game on show, such as the jackal. After all, people in towns seldom see one. We could also have lynxes and wild boars if we can capture them, and of course there are wolves in the mountains.'

'It is certainly an idea, Your Majesty,' an

official replied. 'At the same time no-one is very keen on hunting in the mountains at the moment.'

'No, I can understand that,' the King said.

'Is there any news of the *Zyghes?*' the offical asked. 'I heard they had retreated from the valleys after Your Majesty's troops attacked them.'

'Yes, but that is not to say that they will leave us altogether.'

Zenka listened with interest.

The *Zyghes*, she knew, were savage horse-thieves who lived high in the mountains in the Balkans.

They moved around and were the terror of the herdsmen in every country because they lived by stealing horses and in doing so sometimes injured or killed the herdsmen who were in charge of them.

She remembered her father saying that they usually chose the horses that were already half-tamed, so that months of labour would be lost overnight apart from the fact that the horses themselves were valuable.

The *Zyghes* were ferociously savage and when they moved in large bands they could terrorise a whole neighbourhood.

They stole from the peasants whatever they wished to eat, their sheep and cattle, and often too took young women away with them who were never heard of or seen again.

She could understand the Karanyans being frightened of the *Zyghes*, and although she had not heard of them since she left Hungary she supposed they were still carrying on their nefarious occupation.

It would, she was sure, need a whole Army of trained soldiers to dislodge them from their secret lairs in the mountains.

'I hope they are gone,' the King was saying, 'but one can never be sure.'

'No, Sir,' the officer said, 'but I am certain Your Majesty's prompt action in tackling them so quickly and in such strength has taught them a lesson they will not forget.'

'We can only hope so,' the King replied. 'We have a dozen of them prisoner and they will be tried next month.'

As they drove back towards the city Zenka asked:

'Tell me about the *Zyghes*. I remember what trouble they caused Papa, and how angry it made him when some of our best horses were stolen from the Steppes again.'

'They have grown more daring in the last few years,' the King replied, 'and now they move in a band of several hundreds. We were not troubled with them last year, but they created havoc in Serbia and there were reports from Bulgaria which were extremely disturbing.'

'And now they have come to Karanya,' Zenka said. 'It was clever of you to take some of them prisoner.'

'Unfortunately not very many,' the King replied, 'but I think one of them at any rate is a man of importance. If he is hanged, it should deter the *Zyghes* from raiding our country again.'

'I suppose your fight with the *Zyghes* was the reason why you did not attend the Queen's Golden Jubilee,' Zenka said.

'It was one reason—or shall I say an excellent excuse?' the King answered. 'Quite frankly, I had no wish to waste my time with so many other crowned heads or add my plaudits to the general chorus.'

He spoke scornfully and Zenka said:

'It was an interesting and rather moving occasion. The Queen was really magnificent, but then of course she always is.'

'Of course,' the King replied, 'and so awe-inspiring that I am quite certain poor Bertie as well as the rest of her relations were trembling in their shoes.'

'You were notable by your absence,' Zenka said almost sharply.

'I cannot imagine anybody missed me,' the King retorted, 'and I suffered quite enough boredom when I visited London last year.'

'When you were extremely unkind to Wilhelmina of Prussenberg,' Zenka said, wondering what he would reply.

He looked puzzled.

'Wilhelmina of Prussenberg?' he asked.

'Who is she?'

'The "fat little Frau" you asked someone to prevent making you feel worse than you felt already!'

'How do you know that?' the King asked. Then he added almost ruefully:

'Are you telling me she overheard what I said?'

'She understands Karanyan.'

'Good Lord! I had no idea of that! Was she angry?'

'Extremely hurt. She likes Kings. She wants to marry one.'

'Well, thank God it is not me!' the King exclaimed.

'The Queen might easily have sent her in my place,' Zenka said.

'If she had, I would have handed Wilhelmina over immediately to the *Zyghes!*'

Zenka could not help laughing.

'Is that the fate that awaits me if I offend you?'

'Maybe.'

'Then I warn you if you do I shall make

myself their Ruler and lead them against you in battle...a modern Boadicea!'

He glanced at her with amusement in his eyes.

'I really believe you might,' he said. 'You are a very intimidating woman. I assure you last night I was really nervous in case you fired that pistol at me. I am damaged enough as it is.'

He was teasing her, Zenka realised.

'Wilhelmina told me that you were deformed and limped,' she said. 'I can see the scars on your face, but you appear to walk without any difficulty.'

'I damaged my leg quite badly last year,' the King answered, 'but now it only aches— and I suppose I do limp when I am tired.'

'She certainly gave me a very depressing picture of you.'

'And now you have met me?'

'I find you are not as black as you were painted,' she answered lightly. 'I expected you to look something like the wicked Richard of Gloucester.'

'In which case, if you annoy me I shall undoubtedly murder you,' the King said.

'Then I shall keep my "pop-gun", as you call it, always at my side,' Zenka replied. 'I might have brought it with me to-day in case you fed me to the bears.'

'Judging by the way they were behaving with you,' the King answered, 'I think they would merely cuddle you to death.'

He spoke with an indifferent note in his voice which made Zenka feel sure that whatever the bears might do he himself had no wish to cuddle her or touch her in any way.

When she started to dress for dinner she found herself wondering what Nita Loplakovoff would look like.

At least after she had seen her she would know the type of woman the King admired, and that, she told herself, would be extremely interesting.

The King of course would have no idea that she had ever heard of Nita Loplakovoff in connection with him, and she supposed that if they were behaving as a normal husband and wife would do on their honey-moon he would not be taking her to see his mistress dance.

'It is the sort of thing people would expect him to do,' she thought, 'so no-one would be surprised.'

It struck her that in a way it might endear her to the people of Karanya, who would merely think the King was behaving badly and would therefore be sorry for his poor young wife.

Because it intrigued her to play on the idea she deliberately chose a white gown which made her look very young.

Fanni arranged her hair with long curls falling down the back and instead of wearing a tiara Zenka told the maid to arrange two white camellias on either side of her head.

There was a whole Aladdin's cave of jewellery for her to choose from, she was inform-ed, but instead she wore only her mother's pearls round her neck and a very small unim-portant bracelet of her own round her wrist.

'You look very beautiful, Your Majesty,'

Fanni said when she was ready. 'At the same time you might be a young girl going to your first Communion.'

'Instead of which I am an old married woman of exactly one day,' Zenka laughed.

Fanni opened the bed-room door and Zenka walked slowly down the stairs thinking that this was the first time in her life she had ever dined alone with a man.

They were to eat in a small private Dining-Room which she had already learnt the King preferred to the larger room which could hold hundreds of guests.

They had to take with them to the Theatre an Equerry and a Lady-in-waiting, but since they dined elsewhere in the Palace when Zenka entered the Ante-room she found the King alone.

He was wearing his white tunic although it was not covered with as many decorations as it had been for their marriage, and he looked magnificent and very formal.

She curtsied to him politely and as he moved across the room she saw him taking in every detail of her appearance before he said:

'No jewels? You have only to ask for what you would like to wear.'

'I am sorry if I disappoint you,' Zenka said, 'but after feeling yesterday like someone from "The Arabian Nights" I thought it would be a relief to wear what I actually own myself.'

'I am not complaining,' the King answered. 'I was only hoping that all the resources of the Palace had been explained to you.'

'Everyone has been most helpful,' Zenka answered. 'May I offer you a glass of champagne?' the King asked.

'Thank you,' she said, 'but only very little.'

She took the glass from him, then he raised his as he said:

'I feel I should drink to your first public appearance since you became Queen.'

'Shall I reply that so far it has not been as bad as I anticipated?' Zenka answered.

The King laughed.

'That is not at all the sort of pretty speech you should be making to me.'

'Do you want me to make pretty but insincere speeches?' Zenka enquired, 'or would you rather hear the truth?'

'I have a feeling that is a two-edged question,' the King replied. 'The truth can be very uncomfortable.'

'I should never have imagined you were a coward,' Zenka said provocatively.

'Is it cowardly to avoid trouble—domestic trouble at any rate?' the King asked.

'I have a feeling that like all men you hate a scene,' Zenka said. 'Nagging or jealous wives can, or so I have been told, drive a man to drink.'

'Then I am safe,' the King said, 'for I feel sure you will be neither.'

Zenka resisted the impulse to tell him he was very lucky that she was not jealous, otherwise she would have refused to accompany him to-night to the Theatre. But she felt it would sound undignified to admit she had listened to gossip.

Only as they were seated alone in the charming oval-shaped room which was certainly very intimate and unlike the State Dining-Room did she say:

'Tell me about your Castle. I hear you give very amusing parties there.'

The King looked surprised.

'You heard that? Who has been talking to you about me?'

'You sound surprised,' Zenka said. 'Do you not know by now that everyone talks about unattached and eligible Monarchs?'

'I suppose I might have expected that,' the King said, 'and I am quite certain that everything you have heard about me has been very much to my disadvantage.'

'Do you want me to answer truthfully, or do you want it phrased in pretty words?' Zenka asked.

'The truth!'

She paused, then because she thought it might surprise him she said:

'I was told you gave orgies at the Castle

and I have been wondering ever since exactly what they entailed.'

The King looked amused.

'What do you expect an orgy to be like?'

'I have only read about the Roman ones,' Zenka confessed, 'and I said to somebody when they talked about yours that the Romans apparently got very drunk and took their clothes off, but I thought it would be far too cold amongst the mountains of Karanya to do that.'

The King laughed.

'The Castle is quite warm at this time of year.'

'Then I can expect an orgy?'

'I suppose if I was polite I should promise to try to arrange one,' the King answered, 'but quite frankly I have no inclination for orgies at the moment.'

'How disappointing!' Zenka exclaimed, 'and perhaps now I shall never know what took place.'

'Would you be interested?' the King asked.

He looked at her as he spoke and there was an expression in his eyes that she did not understand.

She wondered if he was shocked at her talking about such things, then she told herself that if he was perhaps it was a good thing.

At least he would not think her dull and spiritless or "an unfledged school-girl" as he had said last night.

Because the subject seemed to have come to an end Zenka said after a moment:

'Would you tell me about Nita Loplakovoff? I hear she was very much acclaimed when she danced in other countries of Europe.'

'So you have heard of her?'

'Yes.'

'I promise you you will be very much impressed by her dancing and by her beauty.'

'You seem to admire her very much,' Zenka replied.

She made her voice impersonal and without looking at the King she realised he gave her a sharp glance.

"I have got him guessing!" she thought. "He is beginning to wonder what I have heard about him and his past behaviour."

Aloud she said:

'I hope I shall have the pleasure of having Nita Loplakovoff presented to me after the performance, I am sure you can arrange that.'

'It might not be possible,' the King said.

Now there was a frown between his eyes and Zenka thought he was thinking about the evening in a way he had not done before.

Because she had no wish for him to change his plans at the last moment she talked of other things, telling him of the Theatres she had visited in London and asking him questions about the sort of theatrical productions which pleased the Karanyans.

As once again the dinner was a short one it was soon time to leave for the Theatre, and Zenka found her Lady-in-waiting and the King's Aide-de-camp were waiting for them in the Hall.

They drove in a closed brougham with a Cavalry escort.

They were cheered by the crowd as they entered the Theatre and escorted with much pomp and ceremony to the Royal Box which was decorated with white flowers.

As they entered the Band played the National Anthem and everybody in the Theatre which was packed from floor to ceiling stood to attention.

Then as the anthem finished everyone burst into loud cheers, there was clapping of hands and Zenka and the King took several bows before they seated themselves at the front of the Royal Box.

Their attendants sat behind them and now as the lights of the Theatre went down Zenka realised that every woman in the boxes facing them and in the stalls of the Theatre was looking at them and trying, she felt sure, to catch the King's eye.

In a box opposite their own Zenka noticed a woman raise her gloved hand and knew it was towards the King.

She looked at him, saw he was smiling and as if he realised she had seen what was happening he explained:

'That is *Madame* Dulcia Rákóczy, the most beautiful woman in Karanya. I will present her to you in the interval.'

'Thank you.'

Zenka inclined her head and she looked across the Theatre at the woman with interest.

*Madame* Rákóczy was dark with, Zenka could see even from a distance, a dazzlingly white skin. She wore a necklace of rubies which seemed to glow like fire and her evening gown was cut very low.

She was bending forward towards the stage and as she did so she glanced under long dark eye-lashes towards the King and Zenka knew without being told that this was one of his mistresses.

"I expect the Theatre is full of them!" she told herself scornfully.

Then the Ballet began and she waited almost apprehensively for the appearance of Nita Loplakovoff.

There was no doubt that the Ballerina was not only an exquisite dancer, but also very beautiful.

She had that indescribable grace with which the Imperial Russian Ballet had set the standard for the whole world to admire and attempt vainly to emulate.

As she danced she made one think of a bird in flight, of a butterfly hovering over a flower, or a star shining in the sky.

Every moment was a poem in itself and Zenka was not surprised that the King did not take his eyes from her when she was on the stage but sat with his opera-glasses watching and watching...

Zenka wondered if the other women in the audience thought she was being neglected.

Without looking she was sure that they were whispering amongst themselves, but she held her head proudly also watching the stage and forcing herself to clap enthusiastically when the curtain fell on the First Act.

'She is wonderful, is she not?' the King asked.

'Of course! Exactly what I expected,' Zenka replied.

Despite every resolution she could not help the cold note in her voice.

It was one thing to dislike the King but quite another to find him enthusing about his mistress in her presence.

Now the King was saying something to his Aide-de-camp and when the young man vanished Zenka knew as they moved into the small room that adjoined the box at the back exactly where he had gone.

There was champagne and sandwiches provided for them and Zenka was listening to her Lady-in-waiting gushing about the performance when the door opened and *Madame* Rákóczy came in.

She was undoubtedly extremely and spectacularly beautiful.

She curtsied to the King with a grace that almost equalled Nita Loplakovoff's, her dark eyes looked up into his and her red lips curved in a mysterious smile like the Mona Lisa's as the King kissed her hand.

'May I present,' he said to Zenka, '*Madame* Dulcia Rákóczy, an old friend whose many kindnesses I can never repay.'

There was something in the way he spoke, the caressing note in his voice, the manner in which he looked at *Madame* Rákóczy which made Zenka freeze.

She acknowledged the lady's curtsey with a frigid bow of her head.

'May I welcome Your Majesty to Karanya?' *Madame* Rákóczy asked in a soft, velvet-like tone. 'I had the great privilege of being present in the Cathedral yesterday and I thought our country had never seen such a beautiful bride!'

'Thank you,' Zenka managed to say.

'I found myself almost weeping.' *Madame* Rákóczy went on, now speaking to the King, 'for the Service was so moving and you, yourself, Sire, looked like one of the Knights whose stories of valour fill our history books.'

Zenka felt her lip curling.

Surely no man, she thought, could want such obvious flattery? "Laid on with a butter-knife" was the way her father would have described it.

But the King was looking pleased and gratified, and he was smiling at *Madame* Rákóczy in such an intimate manner that Zenka thought it was an insult to herself.

"He is lucky I am not a jealous wife," she thought, "otherwise I should throw the bottle of champagne at them both."

The King went on talking to *Madame* Rakóczy and the Aide-de-camp obviously feeling embarrassed that Zenka should be ignored made a few commonplace remarks to which she was obliged to reply.

They heard the bell ring to denote the interval was over and with an obvious reluctance *Madame* Rákóczy made her farewells.

She curtsied to Zenka, then the King escorted her to the door and even for a moment moved outside the box obviously to say a few intimate words which would not

220

be overheard.

Zenka put down the glass she was holding in her hand.

'I am afraid,' she said, 'I have rather a headache.'

'Is there anything I can get you, Ma'am?' her Lady-in-waiting asked.

'No, thank you, but I think I would like to return to the Palace,' Zenka replied.

The King entered as she was speaking.

'I am sure it is very tiresome of me,' Zenka said, 'but I have a headache and it has been rather a long day.'

'Of course. We will go back at once,' the King answered.

'I will order the carriage, Sire,' the Aide-de-camp said and hurried from the room.

'Would you like anything to drink?' the King asked.

'No, thank you,' she replied, 'but there is no need for you to come with me if you prefer to stay.'

'I must take you home first,' the King said, 'otherwise it would cause a great deal of comment.'

Zenka knew he was thinking that people might assume she had disliked seeing one of her husband's mistresses dance, and meeting another in the interval.

That was his problem, she thought. He should not have arranged the evening in the first place.

The Aide-de-camp came back into the room.

'The carriage is waiting for Your Majesty,' he said to Zenka.

'Thank you.'

She rose to her feet, the King offered her his arm, and she took it although for the moment she felt so angry that she had no wish to touch him.

Outside the box there were two officials of the Theatre waiting with anxious faces.

'Her Majesty is feeling tired,' the King explained. 'Will you inform *Madame* Loplakovoff how much we both enjoyed her excellent performance?'

'*Madame* will be very gratified to learn of

Your Majesty's approval, Sire.'

The other official went to Zenka's side.

'I hope Your Majesty will honour us by coming on another occasion.'

'I shall be delighted to do so,' Zenka replied. 'I especially enjoy plays which I am told you often have here.'

'We do indeed, Your Majesty.'

'Thank you for a very pleasant evening,' she said as they reached the hallway.

They were bowed into their carriage, the crowd cheered and they drove off.

Zenka deliberately did not lie back against the seat as if she were suffering from a headache or was even tired.

Instead she talked animatedly to the Lady-in-waiting and the Aide-de-camp.

She meant the King to feel uncomfortable and hoped she succeeded.

When they reached the Palace she heard him say to a flunkey that the brougham was to wait and when they reached the hall she said:

'I feel thirsty. I would like a glass of

lemonade before I retire.'

She was sure the King had intended to say good-night to her immediately, but now there was nothing he could do but follow her into the Salon and wait while a footman fetched the lemonade.

She took the glass from the gold salver and sipped it slowly. Then standing in front of the mantelpiece the King said after a moment:

'I am glad you met *Madame* Rákóczy tonight. You will find her a very interesting person. Her husband died three years ago, and she has not married again.'

That was not surprising, Zenka thought to herself, as she had the King as a lover.

'I was thinking,' the King went on, 'that the Ladies-in-waiting that have been chosen for you are rather old and certainly unattractive. Perhaps you would like to appoint *Madame* Rákóczy to the position. It is quite usual for the Queen to have several extra Ladies-in-waiting for special duties and special occasions.'

Zenka stiffened.

This was intolerable! she thought. How dare he suggest such a thing? How dare he foist his mistresses on her in an official position at Court?

She found herself remembering how Charles II tried to do exactly the same thing to his wife Barbara Castlemaine.

If she recalled the story correctly, the Queen had opposed the suggestion for a long time, and that, she thought, was exactly what she would do.

'May I think about it?' she asked slowly after a little pause. 'My Guardian said that when he became a Duke he was besieged by innumerable people asking him to take on new commitments and to give his name to all sorts of charities and organisations. He told me that he insisted on waiting until, as he put it, he—"played himself in".'

She forced a smile to her lips before she went on:

'I think that the cricket term is rather apt. I shall "play myself in" as Queen before I make any changes or appoint new

Ladies-in-waiting.'

'Just as you wish,' the King said shrugging his shoulders.

'I would wish to have as many friends around me as is possible,' Zenka said. 'Women who like me for...myself.'

'I am sure you will find *Madame* Rákóczy very congenial,' the King said.

Zenka did not answer.

'She is very beautiful,' the King went on, 'and extremely intelligent. She lived in Paris at one time, and has visited London. I can imagine no-one who could assist you more in your new position and whose advice you would be wise to take.'

He was pushing her, Zenka thought, pressing her into accepting a woman he admired and who was quite obviously enamoured of him.

She felt her anger rising almost to a flame inside her.

It was with an effort that she managed to say:

'I will certainly think about your suggestion, but I suppose I am under no compulsion to accept it?'

'No, of course not,' the King said, 'but you are very young and if you do not think it rude, may I say that there are a lot of things for you to learn.'

'Name some,' Zenka said and now there was no mistaking that her tone was defiant.

The King made a gesture with his hand.

'I would not like you to think I was finding fault.'

'If you have anything to criticise please say so,' Zenka said rising to her feet. 'If there is one thing I really dislike it is veiled innuendos.'

'I assure you I was just speaking generally,' the King said. 'Surely at your age you cannot expect to know everything?'

'It depends what I am expected to know,' Zenka said, 'and if you are so keen on having *Madame* Rákóczy in the Palace you can appoint her as one of your Aides-de-camp. I am sure she would fill the position most admirably.'

She did not wait to see the King's surprise at her rudeness, but merely walked out of the Salon and slammed the door behind her.

She ran upstairs and only as she reached her bed-room did she realise that she had lost her temper and wondered what he would think about it.

"It is his fault!" she thought. "He is behaving abominably and the sooner he realises it the better!"

'What has happened, Your Majesty? Why are you home so early?' Fanni asked.

'I am tired and I want to go to bed,' Zenka said like a petulant child.

Fanni undressed her in silence, then withdrew saying good-night in her usual manner.

In the darkness Zenka buried her face in the pillow and thought that she was behaving badly.

'But not as badly as the King,' she excused herself.

He was abominable! Wilhelmina was right in everything she had said about him.

He would be with one of his mistresses by now, she thought. She only hoped he enjoyed himself.

She felt herself seething with fury, but she was not quite certain how she could pay him out or how she could get even with him.

"I knew he would be hateful!" she thought, "and I was absolutely right!"

At the same time her anger made her want to cry. She had no-one to turn to, no-one to talk to.

She thought of the Thief who had kissed her and wondered if she should have suggested running away with him.

She could have been his assistant in crime.

She wondered what he would have said if she had suggested it. Then she remembered his kiss and thought that even if they had had a year or a month together before they were caught and imprisoned it would have been worth it.

Anything would be better than being humiliated by a man she had married against her every inclination, who undoubtedly hated her as much as she hated him.

She thought of the future and felt afraid.

The Duchess and Wilhelmina were wrong. There were no compensations in being a Queen, not if it was to be like this, alone in a great Palace without a friend or anybody to care for her while the King was consorting with the women who adored him and looked at him with dark worshipping eyes as *Madame* Rákóczy had done.

'If only I had something or someone to love,' Zenka thought.

She remembered the softness of the bear she had held in her arms and somehow because it had been so soft and cuddly she found the tears coming into her eyes.

She wiped them away with her hand.

'I am not going to cry,' she told herself proudly. 'I have to fight and go on fighting the King until I defeat him. I hate him and will make him suffer as I am suffering!'

'Then what will happen?' she asked and could find no answer.

# CHAPTER SIX

Zenka stood at the window and looked out onto the mountains.

Every morning since she had come to Tisza they seemed to become more beautiful than they had been before.

Never had she imagined that a Castle could be set in such exquisite surroundings or that the snow covered peaks and the flowers in the valley would have an enchantment which exceeded even the memories of her home in Vajda.

'It is so beautiful!' she said now aloud.

'Indeed it is, Your Majesty!' Fanni answered, and added, 'but your bath is ready.'

Zenka did not turn from the window.

'I can see two eagles against the morning sky,' she murmured almost to herself.

'Let us hope they will not bring further

bad luck to His Majesty,' Fanni said.

'Bad luck?' Zenka asked.

She turned from the window.

'What do you mean...bad luck?'

'Has His Majesty not told you how he received the scars on his face?' Fanni asked in surprise.

'No, he has not mentioned it,' Zenka replied.

'It was fortunate that His Majesty did not lose an eye,' Fanni said. 'But his bravery will never be forgotten by the people of Tisza.'

'Tell me what happened,' Zenka said insistently.

As she bathed in the scented water Fanni began her story.

'It was one day in the Spring, Your Majesty, and the eagles were nesting, and as usual when they have young they are very bold.'

Zenka was listening attentively and Fanni continued:

'The herdsmen are always careful to protect their young lambs in every way they can, and perhaps because they had been extra vigilant the eagles were hungry and instead of taking a lamb one swept down and carried off a baby.'

'A baby?' Zenka exclaimed in surprise.

'It has been known to happen,' Fanni said, 'but this year it was a very special baby because the mother to whom it belonged had married when she was quite old and there had been great rejoicing when she gave birth to a son.'

'I can understand that,' Zenka murmured.

'She put the baby out in the sun-shine on the door-step of their cottage which was high up the hill, as high as the Castle.'

Zenka could guess what happened and Fanni related how the eagle had taken the baby from its wooden cradle and flown away with him towards the mountains.

The mother, distraught with horror, had rushed shrieking out into the roadway and at that very moment the King came riding by with some of his friends.

'When he saw what had occurred,' Fanni continued, 'he called together the best climbers in the village and they set off for the mountains.'

'The King climbed with them?' Zenka asked.

'Of course! His Majesty is an excellent mountaineer. In fact even those whose livelihood it is say he is as good, if not better than they are.'

'I had no idea,' Zenka exclaimed, anticipating the end of the story.

'The King climbed the last bit alone,' Fanni related. 'He would not let anyone go with him. He just told them to keep the eagles alert and watchful.'

'Why did he do that?' Zenka asked.

'So that they would not kill the baby. The eagles will not eat while they are disturbed or on guard.'

'I understand,' Zenka said, and Fanni continued:

'His Majesty reached the eagles' nest and the eagle attacked him. He managed to kill it, but not before it had clawed at his face, making the deep scars you see there.'

'It must have been terrifying!'

'It must indeed!' Fanni said, 'and you can understand, Your Majesty, that they could not shoot the eagle because the nest was partially concealed from the sight of those below.'

'But the King brought the baby to safety?' Zenka asked.

'His Majesty climbed half-way down the mountain,' Fanni answered, 'then because the way was so steep he lowered the baby on a rope.'

She paused before she went on:

'It was then that another eagle, the mate of the one that had been killed, attacked His Majesty and although it was shot down it forced him to lose his foothold and he fell.'

'So that was how he hurt his leg!' Zenka exclaimed.

'His Majesty was very badly injured,' Fanni answered, 'in fact he was laid up for several months.'

"That would have been before he came to England," Zenka thought to herself.

She felt ashamed that she had assumed that the King had received his scars from a jealous husband.

She could imagine how grateful the mother was to retrieve her baby and she could understand now the look almost of adoration that she had seen on the faces of the people of Tisza when the King moved amongst them.

She had been at the Castle now for four days and she had found that to ride the King's magnificant horses was one of the most exciting things she had ever done in her life.

Some were only half-trained and he had promised her that to-day they would start to break in those which were still wild and fought against being ridden.

She had, as she intended, proved herself an outstanding rider and she felt elated when the King said:

'I can understand now why you are proud

of your Hungarian blood. No-one but a Hungarian could ride as well as you do.'

Ever since they had come to Tisza he had been, she thought, kinder and in some ways quite different from his behaviour in Vitza.

There were times however when quite unexpectedly he seemed to become cold and indifferent and would either say something which hurt her or ignore her in a way which left her bewildered and lonely.

Yet they talked as she had never talked to a man before and found surprisingly a great many things in common.

Zenka had always adored pictures and music; she found the King was very knowledgeable on both those subjects.

He was remarkably well read and she would lie awake at night planning a duel of words with him so that she could perhaps defeat him in an argument.

It was something she had never been able to do in the past and she found it fascinating. Yet she was always afraid that the King might find her boring and resent the time he must stay at the Castle away from his mistresses.

She wondered what he talked about with *Madame* Rákóczy and Nita Loplakovoff.

Then she told herself that because they were so beautiful and attractive there was no need for serious conversation and instead he would be making love to them.

She decided that nothing and nobody would persuade her to appoint *Madame* Rákóczy as a Lady-in-waiting.

She knew she could not bear to watch her day after day making eyes at the King or hear the caressing note in his voice when he had spoken to her at the Theatre.

What surprised her was that there was so much to do at Tisza.

There was not only the riding but also the walks twisting up the sides of the mountains from which there were stupendous views. She and the King climbed the paths together accompanied by his dogs.

There were four of them which followed him wherever he went and he said they were never properly exercised except when he was at the Castle.

Zenka had always loved animals although she had never possessed a dog of her own.

She longed to ask the King if she might have one but thought that he would say as he had about the bear, that it might damage the furnishings in her room at the Palace.

Yet the castle was as beautifully decorated as the Palace at Vitza. Here her bed-room was very different, but it seemed as lovely with its white carpet and heavy white curtains as the mountains outside.

All the colour in the room was centred on the huge four-poster bed which was carved by native craftsmen with every alpine flower depicted and painted in its true natural colours.

Never had Zenka imagined that anything could be so attractive, and she would lie in bed and look at the two great posts in front of her, picking out the flowers she recognised.

The Sitting-Rooms also of the Castle were

original in their design and decoration. The King had utilised native rugs with their oriental colours in a way that had a charm that was original and almost indescribable.

In changing the Castle from the austere, cold place it had been in his father's day, he had not forgotten the garden.

It was a complete contrast to the formal gardens of the Palace in Vitza.

Here the wildness of the rocks, the alpine shrubs and the cascades which poured down from the snows all helped to create a picture which was so exquisite that Zenka felt her whole being respond to it.

It was hard to think of or imagine the orgies that she had been told took place in the Castle.

There was something so fairy-like and so peaceful in the atmosphere of it that she began to think it was just one of Wilhelmina's spiteful falsehoods.

It was however, easy to imagine the King making love to the graceful Nita Loplakovoff by the cascades or kissing the beautiful

*Madame* Rákóczy in the Sitting-Room with its large windows from which one could see for miles over the valley.

'I hate them both!' Zenka told herself.

Having finished her bath she started to dress quickly because she knew the King was always punctual and would be waiting for her with the horses.

She put on one of her attractive summer riding-habits that she and the Duchess had bought for her trousseau.

Of a thin material it was the green of an emerald, trimmed with a frogging of white braid. It was very smartly cut and Zenka was aware that it gave her a perfect figure with a tiny waist.

She felt romantic when she was seated on one of the King's large stallions and she knew that her hat with its gauze veil which floated behind her made her hair seem more fiery and her skin whiter than usual.

Fanni gave her her riding-gloves and she left her bed-room to run down the stairs which curled to a hall hung with the heads and horns of the game that the King had shot.

But Zenka had no time to look at anything but the open door through which she could see the horses waiting.

To her surprise however, when she stepped out onto the flight of stone steps which led down to the court-yard she saw that unlike other mornings when they had ridden she was there first.

There were two horses and two grooms were holding them, and she saw with delight that the King had kept his promise.

The horses were not the well-trained animals they had ridden yesterday but were in fact making it hard for their grooms to hold them.

Zenka moved forward and was just about to ask one of the grooms to help her mount when she heard footsteps behind her and thought it must be the King.

She turned round with a smile on her lips to see instead that it was one of his Aides-de-camp.

'Good-morning, Captain Sandor,' she said.

'Good-morning, Ma'am,' the Aide-de-camp replied. 'I regret to inform you that His Majesty cannot ride with you this morning. He has an unexpected visitor who has arrived from Vitza and he asked me to convey his deepest apologies.'

'How annoying!' Zenka murmured, her eyes on one of the horses which was bucking and trying to rear.

'His Majesty hopes you will not cancel your ride, Ma'am,' Captain Sandor went on, 'and has asked me to send for the horse you rode yesterday. He also wishes you to be accompanied by an escort.'

'An escort?' Zenka exclaimed in surprise.

'Yes, Ma'am.'

Zenka's lips tightened.

'I have told them they will be required,' Captain Sandor said, 'and Lieutenant János will be in charge.'

'I am quite prepared to allow Lieutenant János to accompany me,' Zenka said coldly, 'but I see no reason why there need be anyone else. As you know an escort will restrict the pace at which I wish to ride.'

'They are all extremely experienced horsemen, Ma'am,' Captain Sandor answered.

He glanced towards the entrance to the stables, but there was no sign of anyone and Zenka walked resolutely towards the horses.

She patted the neck of the one that was being so obstreperous and as she did so said in a low voice to the groom:

'Help me into the saddle.'

He obeyed her and she was mounted before Captain Sandor realised what was happening.

'There is another horse coming for you to ride, Ma'am,' he cried moving towards her.

'Too late, I cannot wait,' Zenka replied and rode off before he could say anything more.

She had heard him shouting orders to the groom she had left behind, then she was concerned with trying to keep the animal she was riding under control.

It was not easy and she knew the best thing she could do was to give the horse his head and ride some of the devil out of him.

Accordingly she went quickly down the winding path which led from the valley up to the Castle and once there started to gallop over the rough grass.

She had ridden for nearly half-a-mile before she looked back and saw with satisfaction there was no sign of her escort.

Then with a smile on her lips she urged her mount to gallop on, knowing at the pace she was going it would be almost impossible for anyone to catch her.

Only when finally the horse had galloped off some of its rebellious exuberance did Zenka think resentfully of the way in which the King had disappointed her at the very last moment.

Who could be this visitor from Vitza? she wondered, and knew the moment Captain Sandor had spoken that she suspected it might be *Madame* Rákóczy.

She felt a sudden fierce anger that anyone,

especially one of the King's past loves, should intrude on what was supposed to be their honeymoon.

Only a woman would be insensitive enough to do so, for she felt quite sure that the Prime Minister and the other officials she had met at Vitza would not intrude.

'It is *Madame* Rákóczy!' Zenka said to herself. 'I will not have her in the Castle! I will not allow the King to entertain her!'

Even as she spoke she thought helplessly that if that was what he wanted there was nothing she could do about it.

Because she was angry Zenka used her spur on her horse and flicked him with her whip.

He responded by setting off once more in a wild gallop, and Zenka knew that for the moment he was out of control and she could not stop him.

She felt however that the headlong rush was echoing what she was feeling inside herself.

She wanted to get away, she wanted to put

the greatest possible distance between herself and the King, because for the moment she hated him as she had hated him before with every nerve and fibre of her being.

It was nearly an hour later when she realised that having given her horse his head she now had no idea where she was and was lost.

She was far beyond the valley which lay just beneath the Castle and now she found herself moving between great volcanic rocks and had the idea that she was far higher up the side of the hill than she had been before.

She turned in what she thought must be the direction from which she had come but was not even certain of that.

The mountain peaks loomed high above her, silhouetted against the blue sky.

She could not even be certain they were the mountains she had seen before.

'If I ride on,' she told herself, 'I may find someone to direct me back to the Castle.'

There was no hurry, she thought, and she moved slowly; but it seemed as if the ground was growing more rocky every moment and she was afraid of her horse going lame.

Then suddenly—so unexpectedly that she had to bite back a scream that came instinctively to her lips—a number of men appeared.

They seemed to materialise from behind the rocks and they were all round her bringing her horse to a standstill.

She knew at once who they were, knew them by their round lambskin hats, sleeveless sheepskin coats and the pistols and yataghans which they wore in their belts.

She had seen the *Zyghes* before and once seen it was impossible to forget them.

'What do you want?' she asked in Karanyan.

They did not answer her but started to talk excitedly amongst themselves.

Zenka was frightened, but she knew it would be a mistake to show it.

'I am lost. Please tell me the way to Tisza,' she said, then realised she had made an even worse mistake.

At the name of Tisza they talked to each

248

other even faster, their black eyes sparkling, their teeth showing white under their long moustachios as they spoke in a language that at first she found impossible to understand.

Finally she recognised one or two words and said, this time in Hungarian:

'Kindly let me pass. I am in a hurry to return home.'

There was silence for a moment after she had spoken. Then one man who seemed to be a little older than the rest answered her in a mixture of Hungarian and Albanian that she could just understand.

'You are the Queen.'

Zenka was about to deny it, then she thought it would be a mistake to lie.

'Yes, I am the Queen,' she answered. 'Now move out of my way.'

The men made what sounded like a whoop of joy, then they were leading her horse by the bridle and there was nothing she could do but sit proudly in the saddle and wonder despairingly what would happen to her.

* * * *

It was many hours later before Zenka was alone and as she crouched on some straw in the darkness of a cave she was cold and knew that long before the night was passed she would be colder still.

The *Zyghes* had thrown a blanket and one of their shaggy sheepskin cloaks on the ground beside her, but she felt they were as dirty as they were themselves, and she shrank from even touching them.

Yet she knew that as the night progressed she would be obliged to do so.

She realised how foolish she had been riding without an escort, when finally after they had climbed the side of the mountain for a long time they came to where the main band of the *Zyghes* was camped.

It was a narrow opening between the steep sides of two mountains and Zenka realised it was completely hidden from the valley.

There were, she thought, about a hundred men besides those who had captured her, and she was taken in front of their Chief who was, she had to admit, a very impressive-looking figure.

He wore an elaborate costume of crimson covered in embroidery, the round hat he wore was of fox and his boots were of red leather.

He looked like a character out of an Opera, but his appraising eyes beneath his bushy eye-brows were hard and he looked at Zenka with a contempt which made her want to cry out in fear.

She had been forced to dismount and the Chief towered above her so that she felt very small and ineffectual, but somehow she managed to face him defiantly.

'My men tell me that you are the Queen,' he said, speaking a broken Hungarian that it was just possible for her to understand.

'Yes, I am the Queen,' Zenka answered, 'and your men had no right to bring me here.'

A faint smile curved the Chief's lips. Then he said:

'The King has my son. It is only right that

251

I should have his wife.'

'Your son?' Zenka questioned.

Then she remembered how the King had said that among the *Zyghe* prisoners who had been taken he thought one of them was of importance.

Now she knew there was no chance of the *Zyghes* releasing her whatever she might say.

The Chief was obviously thinking what he should do. Then he said:

'You are our prisoner. When my son is freed, then you will be free too. Give me something to show the King that you are in our power.'

Zenka wanted to refuse, then she thought that at least the King would know what had happened to her.

She pulled a handkerchief from her pocket but the Chief shook his head, so she unclasped a narrow gold bracelet which she wore round her wrist.

She held it out to him and he took it from her saying:

'To-day I take bracelet. To-morrow if my son is not released we will send the King one of your ears. The following day a finger, or perhaps your nose!'

Zenka made a little sound of sheer horror.

Then the Chief said something she did not understand which made all his men laugh, cheer and make remarks that Zenka was certain were, if she could have understood them, degrading insults.

She was forced to sit down and listen to the *Zyghes* crowing over their cleverness in taking her prisoner. The men came up one after another to look at her and make remarks about her appearance that made her wish that she could strike the smile from their lips.

They were dirty and reeked of garlic and in a way it was a relief when after they had eaten they decided to put her for the night in a cave high up on the mountain.

The Chief pointed it out to Zenka and she thought in terror that she would never be able to climb so high.

There were many caves in which she realised the *Zyghes* slept or used when the weather was bad, but high above them all there was a small opening which it seemed to Zenka was completely inaccessible.

But the men scrambled up the steep, perpendicular sides of the rocks like monkeys and they dragged her up with them.

Two men pulled her up by the arms, others steadied her from behind, and while she loathed the touch of their hands and the smell of their bodies she was too frightened to protest in case they should let her fall.

She even shut her eyes for the last part of the climb until finally they pulled her into the cave and threw her down on some straw.

She had lost her riding hat soon after she started and she knew without looking down that the men left behind were putting it on their own heads amidst roars of laughter from the others and mocking her.

Now as four men stood beside her in the cave she looked up at them and was suddenly afraid as she had never been afraid before.

It was something in their eyes, something she sensed in their thoughts that she shrank from because it was obscene and terrifying.

Then one of the men spoke sharply and the others who had been standing nearest to her turned away.

'To-morrow,' one of them said, and they all laughed.

Only when she was alone did Zenka realise that she was trembling all over with a fear that was so intense that it was almost like a knife being driven into her body.

For a long time she sat on the straw unable to move. It was growing dark and the *Zyghes* had lit a fire around which they were sitting, drinking and laughing.

The sound of their voices came up to Zenka but they seemed far away and the fire-light only glittered fitfully on the entrance to the cave.

She knew it was a sheer drop from the mouth of it down to where the *Zyghes* were camped and she was too frightened to move, too frightened to do anything but crouch there helplessly, knowing that she had no one to blame for her predicament but herself.

How could she have been so stupid as to ride away alone? And how right the King had been to think that she needed an escort.

She knew now that it had been sheer disappointment that had made her behave so wilfully, and there was another emotion she would not admit for a long time even to herself.

Then in the darkness, as she grew colder and colder, she faced the truth.

She had been jealous; jealous because she thought the King was with *Madame* Rákóczy; jealous because she wanted him to be with her.

Perhaps she would never see him again. Perhaps even if he released the Chief's son the *Zyghes*, who were known to be treacherous, would not keep their word.

They would either kill her or submit her to the even worse fate that she had seen in the eyes of the men who had brought her.

to the cave.

'I must die...I must die!' Zenka murmured desperately and thought how stupid she had been not to enjoy herself since she had come to Karanya.

She realised now that in the last four days she had been happier than she had ever been before in her life, and the reason was quite simply that she had been with the King.

She did not hate him any more. Her hatred had gone, but she had not realised it had vanished until now, when she wanted him with her so intensely that it was almost as if she held out her arms towards him.

Perhaps, she thought miserably, he was not in the least worried by her disappearance and if he was with *Madame* Rákóczy why should he be?

She thought of her beautiful face, her dark eyes turned up to his, her red lips so inviting, so provocative.

She heard the caressing note in the King's voice as he spoke to her and suddenly Zenka covered her face with her hands.

That, she knew, was how she wanted him to speak to her.

Humble in a manner she had never been humble before she admitted the truth.

Inexplicably, unbelievably, she had fallen in love with the man she hated, the man who had married her against his own inclinations, the man who thought of her as merely an unfledged school-girl.

She could remember all too vividly the manner in which he had said so scornfully that if he had had a choice he would not have married anyone who knew nothing of the world and certainly nothing of the things he found amusing.

It was *Madame* Rákóczy whom he found amusing, and Nita Loplakovoff.

'The sooner I die the better! There is no reason for me to live!' Zenka cried and went down into a hell in which the only thing she could think of was that if she had not been so stupid she could have been with the King now.

He might not want her—he might prefer

to be with *Madame* Rákóczy—but at least she could see him and listen to him talking to her.

But instead what did the future hold?

It was so cold that Zenka could feel her teeth chattering, and she told herself that unless she wished to be frozen stiff when the morning came she would have to wrap the cloak around her shoulders and cover her legs with the blanket.

She tried to pull some of the straw loose but it seemed matted together. She was sure this was because it was dirty and felt sick at the idea of lying down where any of the *Zyghes* had lain.

But her fingers were stiff with cold and her nose no longer seemed to belong to her and reluctantly she put out her hand to feel in the darkness for the cloak.

The light from the fire below had died away and so had the voices of the *Zyghes*. She thought now they would be sleeping, getting themselves ready for the morrow when they would be robbing and perhaps killing the people in the valley below.

They had eaten a stew for supper and because Zenka was hungry she managed to swallow a few mouthfuls. She recognised it as being young lamb roughly cooked, but actually surprisingly appetising.

She had however been too frightened and unhappy to eat much.

She had been so vividly conscious of the men around her, but now she thought that one of the reasons she was so cold was that she had hardly had anything to eat since breakfast.

'I must keep warm,' she told herself.

Just as her hand came in contact with the cloth and she was pulling it towards her she saw a sudden darkness obscure the opening of the cave.

Although there was no longer a flicker from the fire below to touch it with a golden gleam the stars had come out, and though there was no moon they were brilliant in the darkness.

Now they were obscured and Zenka could

no longer see them.

For a moment she could not think what had happened, then there was the faint sound of a foot moving on stone and she realised there was a man at the entrance to the cave.

She was so frightened that for a moment she could not breathe.

Then as he moved towards her, dark, enormous and menacing, she parted her lips trying to scream but her throat contracted with terror.

Then suddenly there were arms around her and as the first sound came out in a croak it was smothered by lips that came down on hers and silenced her.

For a moment she thought wildly that it was the Thief who had kissed her, then as she felt herself held in a bearlike grip she knew it was the King.

She did not know quite why she knew it. She was just aware that it was him and while his lips were still on hers she could see the outline of his head silhouetted against the stars.

He must have realised she was no longer rigid with fright for he raised his head and said softly, so softly she could hardly hear:

'Do not make a sound. Do not speak.'

She was so glad to see him that she clung to him convulsively, hiding her face against his shoulder.

He drew her towards the entrance to the cave, then she felt his hands tying a rope round her body and fastening it so that she was close against him.

He put her arms round his neck and carrying her to the very edge of the cave he pulled at the rope which hung down from above.

Afterwards Zenka could never remember the long, dangerous struggle to the summit of the mountain. She felt herself and the King being drawn upwards and with anyone else she would have been desperately afraid.

As it was she shut her eyes and thought that his arms were the most secure and comforting thing she had ever known.

He was there, there when she needed him

most, there when she had been so afraid, and he had come to save her.

There were moments when she felt her body being scraped against the sharpness of a rock, when the King's arms hurt her and she knew he was having to strain every nerve to get them both to safety.

But she was no longer afraid. Nothing mattered. Nothing was of any importance except that he was there and she was close against him.

Her lips were warm from his kiss and her body glowed with warmth because he was close to her.

She knew he had only kissed her to prevent her making a noise, but because she loved him it had been a wonder beyond description.

It was the second time a man had touched her lips.

She supposed that she had first thought it must be the Thief who kissed her because he was the only man she knew who could have accomplished the feat of reaching her cave.

Instead it had been the King—a climber with such expertise that he had undertaken a task which even the most experienced mountaineer would think impossible.

'He is wonderful!' she told herself and pressed her head closer against him.

Only when they reached the top of the mountain did she realise what a long way they had been pulled upwards and how long it had taken.

Now having reached the summit they had to descend on the other side.

There were a number of men who had been handling the ropes, but no-one spoke. The King freed Zenka's arms from around his neck and now she was roped between four men, two in front and two behind.

It was frightening, Zenka thought, to realise how high they were and how steep and barren the rocks over which they had to descend.

There was only the light of the stars and once or twice she found herself hanging between the King and the men below her, her

264

feet in the air and only the toughness of the rope between her and destruction...

Then there were horses, soldiers and the anxious face of Captain Sandor.

Still no-one spoke and Zenka realised that the King had imposed an utter silence on everyone.

It would be easy, she knew, for the *Zyghes* if they learnt she had escaped to shoot at them from above, and she looked back apprehensively at the high mountain down which the King and the mountaineers had brought her.

She thought she would be helped onto a horse, but instead the King mounted one, then held out his arms and Captain Sandor lifted her up to him.

He set her on the front of his saddle and Zenka turned her face and hid it against his shoulder.

His arms held her close, then they were off, moving slowly between the rocks on a path which was little more than a goat-track which brought them down into the valley.

Zenka did not look where she was going. She was only so thankful that she was safe, that she was with the King and that tomorrow there would be no danger of her losing an ear!

At last they reached the valley and began moving quicker, although Zenka knew the King was deliberately holding his horse in check so that she would not find the manner in which they were travelling too uncomfortable.

She would not have cared, she thought, how roughly she was treated or even if she was hurt. All that mattered was that she was safe from the *Zyghes*, safe in the King's arms.

She felt the King draw his horse to a standstill and now for the first time he spoke.

'Are you all right? Those devils did not hurt you?'

She raised her head from his shoulder and found the lights from the door of the Palace were streaming out golden and welcoming.

'You have...saved me!' she said in a low voice.

She thought the King smiled at her, then someone was lifting her down from the horse and a moment later the King had picked her up in his arms and was carrying her up the stone steps and into the hall.

She thought then he would put her down, but instead he started up the stairs. She thought she had never known anything so marvellous as to be back in the Castle and to be close to the King, close against his heart.

Without opening her eyes she knew that someone had opened the door of her bedroom and now they were inside.

She felt the King lay her down on the bed and realised he was going to leave her.

Without thinking she held onto him, whispering:

'Do not...leave...me.'

For a moment he was still, then he said quietly:

'Your maid will put you to bed and I will

come and see you later.'

He went from the room and Fanni with exclamations of horror and commiseration was attending to her.

★ ★ ★ ★

Much later Zenka, having had a bath and food to eat, was waiting.

The King said he would come to her and she was quite certain he would not forget.

At the same time she was afraid that he would think it too late and that she would be asleep.

She lay back against her pillows, her red hair streaming over her shoulders.

She had let Fanni leave only two candles alight by the bed and the rest of the room was in shadow.

It was all so warm, beautiful and comfortable, a room she knew, a room in which she felt at home, and the horrors that she had passed through since she had left it were already receding.

She began to fear that the King had forgotten his promise, when the communicating
door opened and he came in.

He was wearing a long dark robe like the
one he had worn on the night of their wedding, and she thought as she saw the scars
on the left side of his face how much she had
misjudged him.

They had been acquired in a deed of daring and brilliance in which he had rescued
a baby as he had rescued her to-night.

Impulsively Zenka held out her hands
towards him. Then as he drew nearer to the
bed she thought that he looked stern and she
said in a low voice:

'I...am sorry. I know it was all...my
fault...and I do not...know how to...thank
you for saving me.'

'How could you have done anything so
foolish as to ride off alone when I said you
must have an escort?' the King asked.

She knew he was angry and she said after
a moment's pause:

'I was so...disappointed that you would

not...come with me.'

'Was that the only reason?'

Again there was a pause before Zenka, finding it impossible to look at him, murmured:

'N. not...entirely.'

'I want to know what else you felt,' the King said.

Perhaps because she was so tired and weak after all she had passed through Zenka told him the truth.

'I was...jealous,' she whispered.

'Jealous?' the King repeated. 'Of whom?'

'I...I thought your...visitor was *Madame*... Rákóczy.'

The King sat down on the side of the bed facing her.

'*Madame* Rákóczy?' he repeated. 'And that made you jealous?'

There was a note in his voice she did not understand and after a moment, as if to excuse herself, she said:

'I could not think of...anyone else who would come from...Vitza when we were

270

supposed to be on our...honeymoon.'

'My visitor, as it happens, was the Governor of the gaol in which the *Zyghes* I had taken prisoner were being held,' the King explained. 'He had discovered that one of them was the Chief's son.'

Zenka shivered.

'The Chief told me that if you did not set him...free he would send you tomorrow one of my ears, the next day a...finger and the day after that my...nose!'

'I thought it was something like that.'

'Is that why you came...yourself to save... me? How did you...know where I was?'

'Fortunately I know these mountains very well,' the King answered. 'I have climbed most of them at one time or another and when Lieutenant János could not catch up with you and they came back to tell me what had happened I had an idea where the *Zyghes* would be camping.'

'It was very...very frightening,' Zenka said, 'but I have no-one to...blame except... myself. Please...forgive me.'

She looked up at the King, her eyes pleading with him.

'I want you to tell me something,' the King said.

'What is...that?'

'Why you should be jealous of *Madame* Rákóczy.'

'I...know how much you admire her...just as you admire...Nita Loplakovoff. They told me that you had...many, many mistresses... but...'

She found it difficult to go on and after a moment the King said:

'I would like you to finish that sentence.'

'There is...nothing more...to say,' Zenka said.

Now unaccountably her eyes filled with tears.

'They are...so beautiful,' she went on in an unsteady voice, 'so...very beautiful and I understand why you...love them...but I want to ask you...something.'

The tears brimmed over and fell down her cheeks.

The King did not move, he just sat looking at her.

'What do you want to ask?' he questioned.

'B. because I am so...alone and have...no-one to love...I would like to have...a baby. You want to carry on the succession...and it would be something...all my own.'

'I think I would have a part in it, too,' the King said. 'Is that really what you want, Zenka?'

He bent towards her and put his fingers under her chin and turned her face up to his.

For a moment because of the tears she resisted him.

'Look at me,' he said. 'Look at me, Zenka, and answer me truthfully.'

It was hard to do as he ordered, but somehow she managed it.

Her green eyes met his and something in his expression made her draw in her breath and feel as if her heart stopped beating.

'I want to know what you really feel about me now,' the King asked. 'I know you hated me, but I think, though I may be wrong, that hatred has gone.'

Zenka could not take her eyes from his, then because he compelled her, because her will had gone and bereft of pride, she found herself saying almost beneath her breath:

'I...love you...I love you!'

For a moment the King did not move, then slowly with his eyes still holding hers he bent nearer.

She knew what he was about to do, felt herself tremble and his lips were on hers.

She gave a little sob of sheer happiness as his mouth was at first gentle, then demanding and insistent.

She felt as if the stars from the sky fell down and covered them both.

She knew that this was what she had ached and yearned for although she had not realised it.

It had not only been loneliness which had made her suffer, but because she had thought the King did not want her.

At first her lips were very soft and yielding beneath his until, as his kisses became more passionate and she felt as if he drew her very heart from between her lips and made it his, something wild and fiery awoke within her.

It was a sensation she had never felt before and she could feel the flames flickering within her.

She knew there was a fire beneath his demanding lips, a fire which she only vaguely understood, but knew was everything she wanted...everything she thought she would never have.

That was how she had wanted to feel.

She was in love and that was what she had been afraid she would never know when she was told she was to marry a man she had never seen.

When finally the King raised his head, she put her arms around his neck.

'I love you!' she whispered. 'Please kiss me...please love me a little...I know now that this is what I wanted.'

'It is what I have wanted too,' he answered, 'for a whole year—ever since I first saw you.'

She was so surprised that she looked at him in sheer astonishment.

'For a...whole year?'

'I fell in love with you, my darling, when I first saw you at Buckingham Palace.'

'I did not...know you were...there.'

'I thought you were the most beautiful, perfect thing I had ever seen in my whole life, but you were so young. I came back to Karanya and told myself I was a fool and much too old for you.'

'But...you loved me?' Zenka could hardly breathe the words.

'When I saw you curtseying in front of the Queen it was as if a light enveloped you and I knew you were what I had always sought but never expected to find.'

'Why did you not ask to meet me?'

The King smiled.

'Because I thought I was an old fool in love with a school-girl.'

'You...meant to...forget me?'

The pain in Zenka's voice was unmistakable.

The King bent forward to kiss her eyes one after another.

'I tried and found it impossible,' he said, 'so I started to redecorate the Palace and the Castle. I had begun some improvements as soon as my father died, but now I knew that everything must be beautiful for you.'

'I did not know...I had no idea.'

'I know that,' he said. 'I was trying to determine whether I should go back to England or go on trying to forget you, when the Prime Minister and the Cabinet begged me to take an English bride.'

'And you suggested it might be me.'

'Not at first,' the King said. 'I resisted the whole idea of marriage even to save Karanya, but when they insisted I knew what the answer must be.'

Zenka waited and after a moment he said:

'It was as if fate had chosen us for each other, and now I had nothing to do except wait for you to arrive in Karanya saving the country and also me from many sleepless nights.'

'Did you...ask for me...actually ask for... me?'

The King smiled.

'I told the Ambassador that I would marry no-one but you, but he was too much of a diplomat to put such a proposition to the Queen Empress. He knew if he did so that she was likely to refuse and produce a candidate of her own.'

'It might have been Wilhelmina,' Zenka said with a smile.

'If it had been, I swear I would not have married her.'

'So what did...you do?'

'The Ambassador was shrewd and clever enough to suggest that only a Princess who knew the Balkans would be really acceptable to the Karanyans.'

Zenka drew in her breath.

'And so Her Majesty suggested...me?'

'I knew there was no-one else who could fulfil all the conditions that the Ambassador and I had thought up together.'

Zenka gave a little cry of delight.

'That was clever...very clever, but nobody told me, and I thought that all you wanted was a body wrapped up in the Union Jack.'

'And now you know I want something very different.'

'You are...quite sure...that you want... me?'

'Shall I make you sure, Zenka?'

She held out her arms and now her eyes were shining like stars and her lips were parted ecstatically.

For a moment the King did not move.

'I ought to let you rest,' he said.

'Please...kiss me,' Zenka breathed. 'I love..you! Oh, Miklos, I love you...so much!'

The King bent forward to blow out the candles, then he got into bed and Zenka felt his arms around her pulling her close against him.

She knew then that this was love as she had always imagined it would be. Love that was demanding and passionate, but at the same time part of the Divine.

A love that was so exciting, so thrilling, that as she felt the King's hands touching her, as his lips came down on hers, she knew that her dreams had all come true.

# CHAPTER SEVEN

Zenka awoke. The sun was shining in golden shafts at the sides of the curtains.

She turned her head and saw that she was alone.

For a moment she lay looking at the pillow that was next to hers, then impulsively sprang out of bed and ran just as she was to the door that communicated with the King's apartments.

She found herself in a small passage and she ran down it to open the door at the far end.

It opened quietly into the King's bedroom where he was standing with his back to her at his dressing-table brushing his hair with two ivory-backed brushes.

His valet saw her first and he moved towards the door saying as he reached it:

'Breakfast will be ready in a few moments, Your Majesty.'

Zenka stood looking at the King seeing that he was wearing only a white lawn shirt and a pair of tight-fitting dark trousers which accentuated the narrowness of his hips and the smallness of his waist.

He was more attractive, she thought, than she had ever imagined a man could be and as if he felt her presence he turned around and saw her.

'Zenka!' he exclaimed.

'I came to...see you,' she said in a very small voice, 'to find...out if what...happened last night was really true...or just a...dream.'

The King smiled.

'If it was a dream then I was dreaming too. Come here and I will convince you it was real.'

She ran towards him and he put his arms round her, feeling her body warm and soft beneath her thin, diaphanous nightgown.

He did not kiss her but looked down into her eyes.

'You look very lovely in the morning, my darling.'

'You had left...me and I was...afraid.'

'Of what?' he enquired.

'That you no...longer loved...me.'

'Do you imagine that is possible?'

'You...might have...found me only an...unfledged school-girl.'

The hurt of what he had said was still deep within her and in the tone of her voice. The King laughed softly before he said:

'I found you very beautiful, very exciting and very innocent.'

He would have kissed her but suddenly she was still. Then she moved from his arms and he let her go, a puzzled expression on his face.

She walked towards the window to stand looking out blindly onto the mountains.

'What is it?' he asked.

'I have...something to...tell you.'

'I am listening.'

Zenka did not realise that because of the transparency of her nightgown her body was silhouetted against the light and the sunshine turned her hair to flaming gold.

The King watched her, an expression in his eyes that no woman had ever seen.

She did not speak and after a moment he said:

'I am still waiting.'

'You may be...angry at...what I have to...say.'

'It is usually you who has been angry with me.'

'I know...but this is different...I do not want to tell you...but I feel I have to.'

'After last night there should be no secrets between us.'

'That is what I feel...but I am still... afraid.'

'Come here and I will convince you that your fears are quite unnecessary.'

She did not move and after a moment she said:

'I do not want to...look at you in case you are as...angry with me as I...think you will be.'

There was silence, then at last she began:
'When the sleeping-car...stopped on the pass into Karanya...something happened.'
'What was that?' the King asked.
Zenka drew in her breath and in a voice that was hardly audible she said:
'A man came...into my...carriage.'
'A man? Who was he?'
'He said he was a Thief.'
She thought the King must be furious and she said quickly:
'I did not...scream because I was...afraid he might be an...anarchist, but then we sat in the darkness...talking.'
'Surely that was somewhat unconventional?' the King remarked.
'At the time somehow it seemed...right for me to do so,' Zenka answered. 'Then when he said he must go I...I gave him a...present.'
'A present?' the King exclaimed.
'It was something I had been made to buy for...you and although I wanted to give it to...him I also felt in...some way I was...

scoring off you.'

'So he had my present!' the King said.

'Y. yes.'

'Is that...all that...happened?'

There was a silence, then Zenka said almost in a whisper:

'H. he...kissed me!'

She waited for the King to speak and as he did not do so she turned round and ran towards him frantically.

'Forgive me...please...forgive me,' she said holding on to his shirt and there were tears in her eyes. 'It was wrong...I know it was wrong...but I could not bear to deceive you.'

'You need not have told me.'

'I know but you said I was...innocent and it was...a lie. I have been...kissed by...someone else.'

There was silence for a moment, then the King said:

'Tell me truthfully—what did you feel when this man kissed you?'

Zenka drew in her breath and he could feel

she was trembling.

'I want to know!' he insisted.

'It was...wonderful,' Zenka confessed. 'Not as wonderful as last night but...it did make me feel as if...I was part of the mountains...and the stars.'

Her voice died away and she added brokenly:

'You have made me tell you...the truth and I know you will think it...wrong...but it felt right...and good...I. I cannot...explain.'

'I think you have explained it very well,' the King said.

Her two hands were on his shoulders and now he felt her fingers digging into him as she said desperately:

'Please do not let it...spoil our love...please ...please!'

The King smiled, then he said quietly:

'I thought you would be pleased to see that I am wearing my present.'

For a moment Zenka did not understand.

He bent his arm and she saw that in the

287

cuff of his white shirt was a gold link which she recognised—a link bearing a "Z" in diamonds.

She stared at it for a moment incredulously, before she ejaculated:

'It...it was you!'

'Do you really think I would allow any other man to enter your sleeping-car?' the King asked.

'B. but you...spoke in French.'

'I have always been told it is the one language which disguises a voice better than any other.'

'You said you were...a Thief!'

'You assumed that I was one and I was in fact stealing a look at my bride because, as I told you, I could not wait for the morrow.'

'Why did you not...tell me who...you were?'

'Because you told me a lot of things I wanted to know.'

She looked up at him wide-eyed and the King went on:

'I knew after we talked together that you hated me and that you resented having to marry a man you had never seen.'

'I did not...say that.'

'You told me without words. I knew what you were thinking, my darling, as I think I always shall know.'

Zenka hid her face against his neck.

'You are not...shocked or angry that I should have let a...strange man...kiss me?'

'If I did not know who the man was, I should be extremely angry,' the King said, 'very angry indeed! And let me tell you, my precious, that I shall be a fanatically jealous husband. If you ever let another man kiss you, I will kill him and undoubtedly feed you to the bears!'

Zenka gave a little choke of laughter.

'You said they would...cuddle me to... death.'

'Then I might do that myself,' the King answered. 'Are you quite certain that you no longer hate me?'

'You know...I love you,' Zenka said, her

voice deepening, 'but the Duchess said I was a...hell-cat, and that was...how I meant to... behave.'

'How you did behave!' the King corrected.

'And you knew what I was...feeling,' Zenka said thinking it out for herself. 'Was that why you...behaved as you did?'

'I had not exactly anticipated that you would have a real revolver in your hand,' the King replied, 'even though you pretended to hold up the Thief with one.'

'You told me you were not...frightened.'

'Any more than I was frightened when you held me at pistol-point in your bed-room.'

Zenka blushed to think of how theatrical she must have appeared.

'Are you quite...certain you did not... mean all the horrid things you said to me?'

'I knew that I both surprised and perhaps intrigued you,' the King answered, 'and *Madame* Rákóczy acted extremely well in the part I asked her to perform.'

Zenka looked at him wide-eyed as he said:

'So you need no longer be so jealous, my

suspicious one, let me also tell you that Nita Loplakovoff has been married for a year to a Karanyan millionaire which is the reason why she has not danced outside this country!'

He saw the light of relief in Zenka's eyes and went on:

'And *Madame* Rákoćzy is to be married in a month's time to my friend the Duc d'Algero. They have had to wait until the Pope annulled his first marriage, after which they will live in Italy.'

'Oh, I am glad...I am glad!' Zenka cried.

She knew that whatever the King might say she would always be jealous of the lovely woman who had once been his mistress.

'So that clears the decks,' the King said, 'and leaves only us—you and me, Zenka.'

'That is all I want,' Zenka answered. 'To be with you and be quite...certain that you... love me.'

'I will make you sure.'

'Suppose...suppose you find that after all the exciting women you have known I am...

dull and do not...understand the things that...amuse you?'

'What will amuse me more than anything else,' the King said, his voice deepening, 'is to teach you, my beautiful wife, about love.'

'That is...what I want to learn.'

'It will not be hard,' he smiled. 'Your red hair, my darling, is like the fire I ignited in you last night.'

Zenka gave a little sigh of happiness.

'Last night was so...wonderful...so perfect,' she said. 'That is why I was...afraid when I woke up, that it was only a...dream.'

'You really found it wonderful?' the King asked.

'More wonderful than I ever...imagined or even thought...love could be,' Zenka answered.

She looked up at him, then her arms were round his neck.

'Love me...please go on loving me,' she pleaded. 'I will be good...I will do...anything you want me to do...b. but I could not...lose you now.'

The King held her closer still.

'You will never lose me,' he said, 'and there are so many things for us to do together.'

'Breaking in your horses for one,' Zenka said, her eyes alight.

Then she added apprehensively:

'It will be...safe? The *Zyghes* have gone?'

'That is something I was just going to tell you,' the King answered. 'Last night after you had ceased to avail yourself of their hospitality the soldiers moved in. I have learnt that thirteen *Zyghes* were killed and twenty wounded. The rest fled into the mountains and I very much doubt if they will come back.'

'That is marvellous news!' Zenka cried. 'I think if I thought they were there lurking behind the rocks I should always be frightened.'

'They have gone,' the King said. 'But the soldiers are making a thorough search. They were extremely skilful last night in the way they approached the camp without the

*Zyghes* being aware of it.'

'I expect you would have liked to be with them,' Zenka said wistfully.

'I had a more important mission to undertake,' the King answered, 'and later I had a battle of my own to fight.'

'Which you...won!' she said softly.

'I shall have to make quite certain there is no resistance left,' the King said pulling her a little closer. 'No rebellious thoughts which I have not yet discovered.'

'You know I am no longer rebellious,' Zenka answered. 'I only...hated you because I had always hoped that the man I...married would be someone with whom I was...in love.'

'And now?' the King said.

'I have married someone I love more than anything in the world! Oh, Miklos, you are so wonderful, so brave, so exactly what I hoped my husband would be like.'

There was a passionate note in Zenka's voice which brought the fire into the King's eyes.

He bent his head to kiss her and as she clung to him the whole room seemed infused with sunshine and a happiness which glittered as if from some celestial light.

When the King set her free she asked tremulously:

'Suppose I had...drowned myself as I thought of...doing before I reached Karanya? Or I had...run away with the Thief and become his assistant? I did think of it.'

'As the Thief said, you steal hearts, and you have stolen mine completely,' the King said. 'If you ever leave me now it would be impossible for me to love again.'

'I could never leave you,' Zenka answered. 'Never! Never! We will make this fairy-tale land the happiest place in the world not only for us but for everyone who lives here.'

'That is what I want,' the King replied, 'and there is no-one who could help me in the same way as you will, my precious little love.'

He kissed her again and now Zenka felt the fire that had risen in her last night burning through her, moving from her lips into her breast.

It invaded her whole body so that she felt as if she was actually on fire and the flames reached out towards the King.

His lips grew more insistent, more demanding and suddenly—so suddenly that she gave a little cry—he toppled her back onto the bed, then lying beside her began to pull her nightgown from her shoulder so that he could kiss her neck.

She vibrated to the enchantment of him so that it was hard to breathe and difficult to speak, and yet in a voice that was hardly her own, she whispered:

'You are...forgetting...darling Miklos, that...breakfast is...ready.'

The King raised his head to look at her.

'Unfortunately,' he replied, 'there is an emergency of State and the only person who can deal with it adequately is the King! Breakfast must wait!'

Then as she laughed up at him he kissed her until everything was forgotten except the flames leaping higher and higher and the wonder and glory of their love which was both very human and also Divine.

The publishers hope that this book has giv
you enjoyable reading. Large Print Books 
especially designed to be as easy to see a
hold as possible. If you wish a complete 
of our books, please ask at your local libr
or write directly to: Magna Print Boo
Long Preston, North Yorkshire, BD23 4
England.